2-14-20

Cronk Family,

Enjoy the adventure! Always believe in your dreams. Dreams come true!

Map of *Robinson Island*

THE SWISS FAMILY ROBINSON
Secret Discovery

TJ HOISINGTON
KYLA HOISINGTON

AYLESBURY
PUBLISHING

Copyright © 2019 by TJ Hoisington and Kyla Hoisington

Aylesbury Publishing, LLC

www.SwissFamilyReturns.com

ISBN-13: 978-0-9846887-1-5
ISBN-10: 0-9846887-1-4

eBook and audiobook editions are available:
eBook ISBN: 978-0-9846887-3-9
Audiobook ISBN: 978-0-9846887-4-6

Cover background illustration by Stanislaf Plonish
Copyright © 2019 by TJ Hoisington

Library of Congress Cataloging-in-Publication Data

1. Fiction 2. Action & Adventure 3. Time Travel 4. Survival

***The Swiss Family Robinson Secret Discovery** is based on **Return to Robinson Island (2015)** written by TJ Hoisington.*

All rights reserved. No part of this book may be used or reproduced or transmitted in any form or by any means, electronic or mechanical, including photocopying, recording, or by any information storage and retrieval system, without the written permission of the publisher, except where permitted by law.

Printed in the United States of America

First Edition
10 9 8 7 6 5 4 3 2 1

To Julia -
Always believe in possibilities.
Your future is bright!

Chapter 1

"Mom! We're going to build a tree house in the backyard!" Zoe called as she and Katie rushed through the kitchen to the back door.

"OK. Be back before dinner!" Mom yelled just before the door slammed shut.

Zoe and Katie ran into the cedar and fir forest at the back of their house and started collecting large branches at the edge of the yard. It didn't take long to get all the big branches before Zoe decided that they needed to move into the woods to find more. Zoe was twelve years old, four years older than Katie, so it was only natural that she took the lead on building the tree house.

"Katie, go over there and find us some more big sticks," Zoe instructed, "and make sure they're nice and straight."

"All right," Katie called back. Zoe was a good big sister. She was confident and adventurous but always played fair and looked out for Katie. Katie admired and trusted her completely, so she didn't mind if Zoe was a little bossy sometimes.

While Katie went ahead searching the undergrowth, Zoe focused on finding the perfect tree. The branches needed to be low so they could climb it easily, but it also needed to be an old tree so that its branches would be thick and strong enough to hold their weight without bouncing them around. She thought she had found the perfect tree a few days ago when she and Katie had been out exploring in the woods, but now that they were back, all the trees looked the same, and she wasn't sure if they were in the right spot.

The girls were so focused on their tasks, they lost track of time as they moved deeper and deeper into the woods.

Zoe finally found a tree that she thought would work and was about to call out to Katie when she turned around and saw her little sister running toward her, a look of pure panic on her face.

"Katie! What's wrong?"

"Bear!" Katie choked out, her breathing coming fast and hard.

"What?" Zoe asked, desperately trying to keep the fear out of her voice as her sister fell into her arms. "Are you sure?"

"Yes!" Katie panted, pointing behind her.

Zoe looked into the forest where her sister had pointed. The forest was calm and still. She was starting to relax when suddenly she heard a branch snap and saw a bush shake.

"Run!" Zoe screamed, grabbing her sister's hand.

The girls ran as fast as they could through the trees, leaves and small branches smacking their arms and faces. Unfortunately for them, in the confusion of the moment, they never considered they were running away from home, not toward it.

Chapter 2

"Over here," Zoe gasped, pulling Katie behind a large tree. The girls collapsed at the base of the tree, breathing hard. They were deeper in the woods than they had ever been before. After a little while Zoe felt calm enough to peek around the massive tree trunk and check the forest for the bear. The wood was still and quiet, but far off in the distance Zoe spied a beautiful deer wandering through the forest, grazing. Laughing, she leaned back against the tree next to Katie.

"Your bear looks an awful lot like a deer," she told Katie, still laughing.

"Are you sure?" Katie asked, her cheeks reddening.

"See for yourself."

Katie cautiously looked around the tree in the direction from which they'd run. She saw the deer stepping carefully through the forest.

"Don't worry about it," Zoe said as Katie slumped down next to her. "Anyone could have made that mistake."

Katie was grateful that Zoe wasn't making a big deal out of the situation. Living so close to the forest, she had seen hundreds of deer. It was absurd that she would confuse such a beautiful, graceful animal with a bear. In fact, now that she was sure that they weren't in any danger, she saw the humor of their situation and started to laugh. The more Zoe laughed, the more Katie laughed too, and it didn't take long before both girls were laughing hysterically.

When their laughter finally subsided, the girls looked around. This part of the forest was unfamiliar to them. As they stood and walked around, they began to realize how big the tree they had been resting against was.

"Whoa," Katie breathed, "look at this tree. We should build our tree house here."

Zoe stood studying the tree with her hands on her hips. "No, this tree won't work for a tree house," she concluded. "It's too tall and the branches are too far up for us to climb without a ladder."

"Too bad," Katie muttered, "this place is so cool."

"It sure is," Zoe said, sitting back down at the base of

the giant tree. Their run through the woods had tired her out more than she realized. After a few minutes, Katie sat down next to her. The girls sat quietly, grateful for the rest.

While sitting with her back against the tree, Zoe picked up a small stone from the ground and tossed it in the air. As the stone arced through the air, it suddenly began to glow a brilliant shade of yellow. Zoe was so shocked by the change, she pulled her hand away before the stone could touch her, and it fell to the forest floor. When the stone landed, it created a ripple effect of dozens of glowing stones surrounding the tree.

Jumping to their feet, Zoe and Katie screamed because of the change that came over the forest floor. The ground was GLOWING!

"What's happening?" Katie shrieked.

"I don't know," Zoe said, stepping back from the tree.

"What is that?" Katie asked pointing to the tree.

Zoe was so preoccupied with the glowing stones on the ground, she hadn't noticed the door that had formed on the tree's giant trunk. The door was the same color and texture as bark, but it was unmistakable. There was definitely a door in the tree.

Zoe couldn't believe her eyes. Things like this only happened in fairy tales. "I'm going to touch it," Zoe told Katie, stepping forward.

"Be careful," Katie whispered, holding on to the back of Zoe's shirt.

Zoe reached out to touch the door and was surprised

to feel . . . nothing. She pushed her hand forward and was shocked when her hand disappeared.

"Look, Katie," Zoe said, gesturing toward the tree. It looked like her hand had been swallowed by the tree.

"Take it out!" Katie screeched.

Zoe pulled her arm back and her hand reappeared. Zoe studied her hand. She wiggled her fingers and then made a fist and released it quickly. Everything looked and felt perfectly normal. Relieved, she laughed and hugged Katie.

Taking courage from her sister, Katie stepped toward the tree. "I want to try it too." It was amazing: just like Zoe's, Katie's hand disappeared through the door. She pulled her hand out again, laughing nervously.

The girls spent the next few minutes taking turns putting their hands through the door, gaining courage each time they did.

"Is this a magic tree?" Katie asked.

"I don't know," Zoe replied, looking at the tree thoughtfully. "I wonder what would happen if we stuck our heads through the door."

Katie wasn't sure that was such a good idea, but Zoe's curiosity was infectious. "Let's try together," she replied, taking Zoe's hand.

"OK," Zoey smiled. "We'll do it on the count of three."

Katie nodded. "One, two, three, go!" the sisters said in unison, and leaned their heads into the door.

The girls never stopped to consider what they might see

on the other side of the door. It wouldn't have surprised them to see the inside of a hollowed-out tree, or to see the forest on the other side of the tree, so it was a complete shock to open their eyes and see a tropical paradise in front of them.

Chapter 3

Zoe jumped back from the tree, pulling Katie with her.

"What on earth was that?" Katie whispered.

"I'm not sure," Zoe replied thoughtfully. It had been only a moment or two, but Zoe was sure she had seen a tropical landscape on the other side of the door. How could that be? It didn't make any sense.

"Katie," Zoe said, turning toward her little sister, "what did you see on the other side of the door?"

Katie chuckled nervously. "I'm not exactly sure, but it looked a lot like Hawaii to me."

"You're right," Zoe agreed. The girls sat quietly for a moment or two, thinking about what had just happened. Then Zoe had a brilliant idea.

"Katie! If Hawaii is on the other side of that door, then we should get Mom and Dad and go on vacation."

"Yes!" Katie squealed, jumping up. "That's a great idea. I wish I had thought of it. Let's go get them now."

"Hold on, Katie," Zoe said, pulling her sister to her side. "Let's make sure it really is Hawaii before we get Mom and Dad."

Katie nodded her head. "Yeah . . . OK. That makes sense."

The girls walked back toward the giant tree with the mysterious door in its trunk. There was no fear or trepidation this time as the girls joined hands.

Zoe looked at Katie. "Are you ready?"

"Yes," Katie replied.

"All right then," Zoe said, nodding her agreement. "Ready, set, go."

This time the sisters were so excited that they practically ran through the door. In fact, they went through the door so quickly, they tripped on the large roots of the tree on the tropical side of the door and fell, scraping their knees.

The first thing the girls noticed was the heat. It was much warmer and far more humid than the forest at home. The second thing the girls noticed was the noise. The jungle trees here were much smaller, with giant leaves that rustled in the warm wind. The real racket, however, seemed to be coming from a flock of tropical birds hidden in the forest's canopy.

Katie looked up in the trees trying to find the chatty birds.

"Zoe, look!" she squealed, pointing up. "Monkeys!"

Zoe looked up and laughed. Sure enough, a couple of long-armed monkeys were swinging through the trees on their way to some unknown destination.

"This place is amazing," Zoe said standing up. "Let's go see if we can find a sign, or something that will tell us where we are."

"Good idea," Katie said, following her sister down a lightly worn trail. "I bet we're in Maui. This place looks just like the hike we went on when we were there on vacation last summer."

"Maybe," Zoe mused, looking through the trees to her left. "Did you hear that?"

Katie and Zoe stood very still, listening to the sounds of the forest. Suddenly they heard happy shrieks followed by a burst of laughter.

"Let's go check it out," Katie suggested, moving toward the sounds.

"OK," Zoe agreed, "but we need to be careful until we know where we are. This might be private land, which means we could be trespassing."

As the girls quietly moved through the dense jungle, the sounds grew louder. They crouched down behind some bushes when the jungle cleared to reveal a river running into a beautiful blue lagoon. The water was crystal clear. There were rocks and cliffs on both sides of the river and surrounding the lagoon. Trees reached over the lagoon like a canopy, and sunlight reflected off the water. It was gorgeous!

There was another loud yell as a young man swung himself

out over the lagoon from a rope tied to the branch of a tree growing out of the surrounding rocks. Two more children were waiting at the tree for a turn on the rope swing. As the young man plunged into the water, cheers erupted from the others in the group. The girls smiled, thinking of the fun they could have here with their family.

Katie smiled and stood, wanting to join in the fun, but Zoe pulled her back down.

"What are you doing?" Zoe hissed. "We don't know who these people are."

Katie frowned and crouched back down. She shifted her weight, trying to find a comfortable position on the ground, and a branch suddenly snapped under her.

The girls froze.

"Do you think they heard that?" Katie whispered.

"I don't think . . ." Zoe was starting to say when a sharp whistle filled the air. The family in the lagoon went completely silent.

"I think we've got company," the old man on the rocks below yelled, standing up.

The silence in the lagoon was deafening as the men in the water hurried to shore and picked up rifles. The women stood up quickly and made their way to the waterfall.

"This is bad," Zoe whispered, looking at the guns.

"Maybe they don't know where we are," Katie suggested.

That hope was crushed when, a moment later, the old man pointed right in their direction and yelled, "Over there!"

"Let's go, Katie," Zoe commanded. "We've got to get out of here right now!"

The girls jumped up and ran wildly up the path toward the tree. It was so large—much larger than all the other trees surrounding it—that they would have recognized it anywhere. When they finally reached the tree, terrified and breathless, they searched frantically for the door in the trunk. They circled the tree several times before they realized the door wasn't there. It had disappeared.

"What do we do now?" Katie cried, tears forming in her eyes.

Zoe knew they had only moments to act before the men would arrive.

"Quick, hide!" she instructed, motioning for her sister to follow her. The girls lay on the ground and folded themselves under the giant roots of the tree. It wasn't a great hiding place, but it was the best they could do. It was the second time in one day the sisters sought safety from the magic tree.

Chapter 4

Lying close together, the girls struggled to control their breathing. Every ragged breath sounded like an alarm announcing their hiding spot.

"Where are they?" Katie breathed. "Do you think they're still looking for us?"

"I don't know," Zoe said, straining to hear any unusual sounds in the jungle, "but we can't hide here forever. I'm going to get up and take a look around. Stay here until I let you know that it's safe to come out."

Zoe unfurled herself from the giant root and crept around the tree. She stayed perfectly still, watching the forest for any movements or sounds that would be out of place. After several uneventful minutes, she began to relax. Maybe they had evaded their pursuers after all. Zoe stood and quietly stretched, allowing the stress from the day to melt away. Now she needed to find the door in the trunk of the tree. She was sure it was there somewhere. She rested her hand against the tree and started to walk around it. Suddenly she spotted a boy on the other side of the trail, watching her.

Zoe froze and locked eyes with the boy. He looked to be about her age, although, unlike her, he showed no trace of fear. Zoe was still staring at the boy when three men materialized out of the forest without making a sound. One of the men was older, with graying hair and deep lines in his face. The other two men were middle aged, like her dad, but their faces were serious as they took in the scene. They were holding rifles, but when they saw that she was a young girl and apparently alone, they relaxed and lowered their weapons. They no longer looked so serious; in fact, they looked friendly, as if they were more accustomed to smiling and laughing than scowling. As the men shifted their rifles to their backs, Katie could see that a young boy about the same age as Katie was standing just behind them.

"Who might you be?" one of the middle-aged men asked.

"And what is that you're wearing?" the older boy asked.

Zoe looked down at her pink Converses, cut-off jean shorts, and neon striped T-shirt. She couldn't help noticing how different her clothes looked from those of the men in front of them. Their clothes were very out of date. In fact, as Zoe looked closer, she realized they looked like actors about to reenact a scene from the Revolutionary War. Their pants fit loosely and their shirts were white and baggy. Their feet were bare, but that wasn't surprising considering they had just come from the lagoon. Zoe's bright shoes and shirt made her feel very out of place, like a tropical bird in Alaska.

"My name is Zoe."

"Where are the others?" the old man asked.

"It's just me and my sister, Katie." Zoe motioned for Katie to join her. She put her arm around her sister and pulled her close.

"How did you get here?" the old man asked, studying her curiously.

"Well," Zoe began, laughing nervously, "you're probably not going to believe this, but we came here through a door in this tree."

"A door? In the tree?" one of the middle-aged men asked.

"Yeah," Katie spoke up, "but it's not there anymore."

The men looked at one another, obviously at a loss for words.

"Who are you?" Zoe asked. "And where are we?"

The older man stepped forward. "We are the Robinsons. You are on an island in the Indian Ocean, not too far from New Guinea. My name is William, but here on the island I'm simply Grandpa."

Zoe and Katie looked at each other, struggling to understand.

"This is my son Fritz and his son Nicholas." The older boy, Nicholas, raised a hand in a friendly hello. "And this," Grandpa said, gesturing to the other young man, "is my youngest son, Francis." Francis nodded hello and smiled at the girls.

"So I guess that means we're not on Maui," Katie said.

"Maui?" Grandpa repeated. "I don't know what a Maui is, but our family came from Switzerland."

"Wait a minute!" Zoe practically shouted. "I know who you are. You're the Swiss Family Robinson!"

"What do you mean?" Fritz asked, obviously confused.

"Do you live in a tree house?" Katie asked.

"Yes," Nicholas answered, "it's really amazing."

"Your family was shipwrecked and you made this island your home?" Zoe asked, excitement shining in her eyes.

"Yes, that is true," Grandpa said, watching the girls with new interest. "You seem to know a lot about us."

Zoe giggled. "Everyone knows about the Swiss Family Robinson. You're famous!"

"Famous?" Grandpa asked.

"Oh yes! Our dad has been telling us stories about your family all our lives. We love hearing how you built your tree house, and how you fought pirates to save your island," Zoe explained.

"It's true," Katie chimed in. "Our dad even wrote a book about your family's adventures."

"A book?" Francis chuckled. "What is there to write about?"

"Being shipwrecked and living on a deserted island is not very common where we come from," Zoe began.

"And neither is living in a giant tree house," Katie added.

Zoe nodded in agreement. "And then you add in pirates, and everyone's interested."

Grandpa laughed. "When you put it that way, it makes us sound like a mighty interesting family."

"And then there's Ernest's adventures at sea," Zoe continued.

"How did you know about Ernest?" Francis asked. "We didn't mention him."

"We told you," Katie sighed, trying not to roll her eyes, "we know all about you."

"Well, it seems that we're at a disadvantage then," Grandpa chuckled.

"I can't wait to tell Dad about this. He'll be so excited." Zoe pulled her cell phone out of the back pocket of her shorts. She tried calling her dad, but there was no connection.

"What is that?" Fritz asked, watching Zoe curiously.

Zoe giggled. "It's my cell phone."

"What's a cell phone?" Nicholas asked.

"It's something we use to communicate with family and friends, but it doesn't seem to work here." Zoe walked around with her phone in the air, trying to find a signal. The Robinsons watched Zoe's strange behavior in confused silence.

Zoe finally noticed the awkward silence and put her arm down. "You've never seen a phone before," she said more than asked.

"Where we live, everyone has cell phones," Katie explained.

The group of men nodded, trying to be polite.

Zoe started to feel a little unsettled. "What year is it here?" she asked.

"We are in the year 1817," Grandpa answered.

"Where we live it's 2019," Katie informed the group.

Again there was silence. Zoe's uneasiness was turning into fear. The door in the tree was gone, and the girls had no way to let their parents know where they were. Worse yet, it would be dark in a few hours and the girls would be alone in the jungle. Zoe was trying to come up with a plan when Grandpa Robinson spoke.

"Well, young ladies, it looks like you'll be staying with us until we can figure things out." Grandpa wasn't sure about the strange story—a door in a tree—but it was obvious that the girls were alone and couldn't be left to fend for themselves. The island was full of wild animals like panthers and wild boars; it was just too dangerous.

Relief flooded through Zoe. She had always been taught to be cautious around strangers, but the Robinsons didn't feel like strangers to her at all. Her dad had told them so much about the adventures of the Swiss Family Robinson that she felt like they were good friends.

"Thank you," Zoe said, "we appreciate your hospitality."

Katie looked at her sister and smiled. "This is going to be awesome!"

Chapter 5

The family and the girls made their way downhill. As they entered the clearing leading into the lagoon, Grandpa gave a sharp whistle. The girls looked at him, startled, but their concern vanished when he smiled at them and winked.

"He's just letting Grandma know that we're here and everything's all right," Nicholas said.

The lagoon looked deserted, but a moment later an older woman and a younger woman holding a toddler on her hip stepped out from behind the waterfall.

"That's Grandma," Nicholas said, motioning to the older woman, "and that's my mother with our baby sister."

Just then, a young boy stepped out from behind the women.

"And that's my brother, Jacob," Nicholas said.

Noticing the young child in the arms of the children's mother, Katie remarked, "Your sister is adorable. Is this Anne?"

"Yes. She's three," said Jacob proudly.

Katie smiled.

"Well, Mother," Grandpa said, taking Grandma's hand, "we didn't find any pirates this time, but we did find a couple of young visitors."

"How lovely," Grandma said, smiling at Zoe and Katie. She noticed the girl's strange clothes and shoes but didn't say anything in front of them. Wanting her guests to feel welcome, instead she said, "I hope you'll be staying for a while. Jenny and I are always happy to have more girls around." She gestured toward Nicholas and Jacob.

"That's true," Jenny said, laughing. "We're a bit outnumbered here."

"Thank you," Zoe said. "We appreciate you letting us stay."

The group made their way down the jungle hillside. Time passed quickly as they discussed the girl's remarkable story. Soon the ground leveled out as they walked into a clearing, and Zoe and Katie stopped and stared.

"Wow," Zoe breathed, taking in the scene in front of her.

"Welcome to Falconhurst," Francis said, smiling.

The girls looked up at what appeared to be a very large and extensive tree house. Several trees were grouped together, although one tree stood out because it was spectacularly large with an enormous trunk. As the group came closer, the girls noticed that there were actually six individual cabins nestled in the branches. An intricate rope bridge connected the trees and a series of stairs connected all the cabins together.

"Our dad told us all about your famous tree house, but it's much more beautiful than I could have ever imagined," Zoe said.

"He even told us how to get up into it," Katie offered.

"Is that so?" Grandpa asked.

"Sure," Katie said. "The big tree trunk is hollow, and inside there's a stairwell that takes you up to the main living area."

The Robinsons were surprised, although they tried not to show it. The door to the stairwell was very well concealed. It was a detail the girls should not have known.

"Well," Fritz said, opening the door in the trunk, "you are very well informed. Let's go on up."

The main living cabin was everything the girls had imagined and more. There was a wood couch with several wood chairs grouped around it. The dining room featured a large, family-size table with benches. The kitchen was ordinary except for a network of bamboo pipes that delivered fresh water into a sink made out of a large turtle shell. It was rustic and charming all at the same time and felt familiar and homey to the girls.

"Jacob! Nicholas!" Jenny said. "Why don't you take Zoe and Katie on a tour of the tree house and let the grown-ups talk for a moment."

Jacob and Nicholas grinned at their mother. "Let's go," they shouted, pulling the girls toward the rope bridge.

A few moments later the children were standing in the center of the rope bridge.

"We're forty feet off the ground right here," Nicholas said as they leaned against the railing, looking down. From their high vantage point, the girls could see the entire establishment the Robinsons had named *Falconhurst*.

Down below, and spread throughout the clearing, they could see several gardens, a guest house, a blacksmith's shop used to make metal tools and implements, a smoke house for preserving food, and several outbuildings nestled on the edge of the jungle. It looked like a tiny village, and the girls loved it immediately.

"You're so lucky to live here," Zoe said, looking at Nicholas.

Nicholas bowed his head and grinned. "If you think that's great, wait until you see the rest of it."

For the next hour the children could be heard laughing and scampering up and down the stairs leading from one cabin to the next. The boys loved having children their own age to play with and enjoyed seeing their unique home through new eyes.

Suddenly a bell rang. "Children!" Jenny called. "It's time for dinner!"

The children made their way down to the main cabin. The large dining table had been set and was full of fresh, colorful tropical fruits, potatoes, a salad, and a savory roast. Zoe and Katie hadn't realized how hungry they were until they saw the table overflowing with food.

Zoe and Katie sat at the table and joined hands with the family. Grandpa began the meal by saying grace and then began passing the platters of food around. Conversation began as the girls were asked what they thought of the Robinson home.

"We love it here," Katie exclaimed, putting a freshly cut piece of papaya into her mouth. Zoe's mouth was already full, so she nodded her agreement enthusiastically.

As the meal was coming to a close, Grandpa cleared his throat. "Earlier, while you were off exploring, we decided that we should go back to your magical tree tomorrow and take a closer look," Grandpa explained, looking at Katie and Zoe. "Perhaps the door only appears at certain times of day, or can only be seen in certain light. In any case, we need more information."

"Sure," Zoe agreed, "that sounds like a good plan."

"That's settled then," Grandma said, smiling. "The men can clean up tonight while Jenny and I get you kids settled. It's been a long day."

Nicholas and Jacob protested that it was too early to go to bed, that they weren't tired at all, but their mother only smiled and led them across the bridge to their family's cabin.

Grandma led Zoe and Katie up some stairs to a cabin not far from the living area. "Grandpa and I thought it would be best if you girls stayed with us tonight," Grandma said. "You'll be sleeping in Fritz and Ernest's old room, which is right next to ours."

Grandma led the sisters into a small bedroom and poured water into a large bowl on a dresser between two beds. She then handed them two small towels to wash up with. It felt wonderful to the girls to be clean after such an eventful day.

"I don't have any nightgowns your size," Grandma said, "but I did find these shirts in a trunk in my room which should work well for tonight."

Grandma left the room for a moment to allow the girls to change into the large shirts, which hung well below their knees. The sleeves were far too long and swallowed their arms completely. When Grandma came back into the room, she was carrying a candle. The sun sets quickly in the tropics, but the girls were so tired they hadn't really noticed. Laughing when she saw how long the sleeves were on the girls, Grandma put the candle on the dresser and took a few moments to roll them up.

Grandma pulled the blankets back and the girls gratefully slipped into bed. The room was cozy and warm and the girls felt safe and secure.

Grandma took a moment to gently brush the hair off the girls' faces. "Try not to worry, my dears," she said softly. "I'm sure everything will work out, and until it does, we're happy to have you here with us."

"Thank you," Zoe mumbled, struggling to stay awake. "You've been so kind to us."

Grandma looked over at Katie, ready to offer her words of encouragement, but she was already fast asleep.

Chapter 6

The girls woke slowly the next morning. Before they opened their eyes, they heard a loud chorus of birds chirping, but it was the wonderful aroma of bacon tickling their nose that got them to their feet. Sitting on the edge of the bed in her oversized shirt, Zoe looked at Katie and grinned.

"It wasn't a dream," Zoe said, surveying their tree house bedroom.

"We're really here!" Katie exclaimed.

Zoe and Katie quickly changed back into their regular clothes and followed the smell of bacon to the kitchen, where Grandma and Jenny were preparing breakfast and baking bread for the day. Baby Anne was safely tucked away in a corner of the room, playing with hand-carved figures of animals.

"Good morning, girls," Grandma said when she saw Katie and Zoe entering the room. "I trust you slept well?"

"Oh yes," Zoe replied. "I don't think I've ever slept so well in my entire life."

Katie shifted her feet uncomfortably. "Mrs. Robinson?" she asked shyly. "Where's the restroom?"

Grandma handed the hot skillet off to Jenny and led the girls to the front balcony. "It's just over there," she said pointing to a small building at the edge of the jungle.

"Thank you," Katie said, relieved.

"We'll be back soon." Zoe led Katie down the giant tree trunk stairwell. The girls quickly made their way to the outhouse, not really paying attention to the other buildings around them. With their task complete, the girls slowly made their way back to the tree house, exploring the buildings along the way. The girls were peeking into the window of one structure when the sound of banging metal startled them. They jumped back from the window.

"What was that?" Katie asked.

Zoe looked at Katie, thinking hard. When she heard the clanging sound again, she smiled. "This is a blacksmith's shop," she answered confidently.

"Blacksmith?" Katie asked. "What does a blacksmith do?"

"A blacksmith heats up metal and then shapes it to whatever shape he wants by hitting it with a hammer," Zoe replied confidently. She had learned all about it on a fieldtrip she took with her class last year to downtown Seattle, but she'd never actually seen it done.

The sisters circled the building to the open door and watched quietly as Grandpa stood in front of an oven, holding a long, narrow piece of metal in the hot embers of a fire. Francis was standing a little ways off at a large metal anvil, holding a piece of red-hot metal with metal tongs in one hand and carefully using a hammer to hit the metal into a flat, rectangular shape.

"Good morning, girls," Grandpa called out, looking up from the fire.

"Good morning," the girls chorused.

"What are you making?" Katie asked.

"We're making a new hinge and door plate for the tree trunk door," Francis said.

"This is hot work," Grandpa said, nodding to the fire, "so we like to get started as early as we can before the heat of the day is at its worst." He took the metal out of the fire and inspected it—the tip was glowing red. He handed the metal rod to Francis, who took it in his gloved hand and started shaping it into a cylinder on the anvil.

Grandpa closed the door to the oven and took off his heavy apron. "We're just about finished here for the day," he said. "Why don't you run on up to the house and let Grandma and Jenny know that we'll be up in a moment."

The girls hurried back up to the kitchen to pass on Grandpa's message. Nicholas and Jacob were in the kitchen, setting the table and playing with Anne on the floor. They had spent the early part of the morning helping their dad water the gardens and tend to the animals, which consisted of chickens, goats, and pigs. The table was set and the food finished when the men made their way up to the kitchen, washed and cleaned from the morning's work.

The family sat around the table enjoying a meal of oatmeal, eggs, bacon, fresh fruit, and guava juice. It was delicious and refreshing and there was plenty for all.

As the meal was coming to an end, Grandpa turned to the girls. "What time do you think you stepped through the tree yesterday?" he asked.

Zoe had looked at her phone when they were on the other side of the tree so she was able to answer confidently. "It was right around four o'clock."

Grandpa nodded. "That gives us plenty of time to prepare," he said.

"Father, can we take Zoe and Katie to the Rock?" Nicholas asked.

Fritz smiled and nodded. "Yes, I think that would be fine, as long as your mother doesn't need any help this morning," he answered, looking at his wife.

Jenny smiled at her sons, whose excitement shone on their faces. "You children go along and have some fun," she replied.

The boys whooped and jumped up from the table. Grandma laughed and looked at Francis. "I think you'd better go along and keep an eye on things."

"Yes," Grandpa agreed. "Fritz and I will put the new hinge on the door while you're gone."

"All right," said Francis, smiling. "I'll make sure the little scamps don't get themselves into any trouble."

"Let's go!" Jacob squealed, pulling on Francis' arm.

The girls followed Francis and the boys down a well-worn path in the jungle toward the beach. After only a ten-minute walk they emerged from the jungle and into a clearing dominated by huge boulders. The boulders were naturally arranged in a circle with an open space in the middle that the Robinsons used to hide in. It was the perfect hiding place because the rocks looked like a solid mass and unless you knew exactly where to look you would never find whoever was hiding inside. Francis walked toward the beach as the children found their way to the secret hiding place.

"This is so cool!" Katie exclaimed, looking up at cotton candy clouds from the middle of the rocks.

"It is cool," Nicholas agreed. "The rocks shield you from the sun so it only gets really warm in here at midday."

Zoe giggled. "She meant that it's very spectacular," she said. "Where we come from, 'cool' means that something is great."

"But that doesn't make any sense at all," Jacob said, a puzzled look on his face.

"You're right," Katie said laughing. "It doesn't make any sense at all."

Nicholas shook his head, bemused. Then he suddenly had an idea. "Follow me," he called out, climbing up the boulders.

The children climbed to the top of the rock formation and

were rewarded with a breathtaking view of the crystal blue ocean. It was the most beautiful beach the girls had ever seen.

"It's so pretty here," Katie said.

Nicholas smiled, proud of his island home.

The children saw Francis walking slowly along the beach and decided to catch up with him. They scampered down the rocks and raced each other down the beach. When they finally reached Francis, they were out of breath but smiling.

"What do you think of my friend over there?" Francis said pointing to what looked like a giant boulder on the beach. The girls were stepping closer for a better look when the boulder suddenly moved.

"Hey!" Katie yelled, jumping back. "What is that?"

"It's a turtle," Nicholas said, laughing at the girls.

"I had no idea a turtle could get so big," Zoe said.

"Most of them don't get as big as my friend here," Francis said, rubbing his hand over the top of the giant's shell.

"That's true," Jacob agreed. "The small ones are much easier to catch."

"What do you do with them?" Katie asked.

"Eat them, of course!" Jacob laughed. "What else would you do with a turtle?"

Katie couldn't believe what she was hearing. She had heard of keeping turtles as pets, but she had never considered eating one.

"You eat them?" she asked, incredulous.

"Sure," Nicholas replied, throwing a rock into the ocean.

"They're delicious."

The awkward conversation would have continued, but they were interrupted by Francis. "Who wants a ride?" he asked.

"I do!" Katie called out, jumping with excitement. She may have thought eating a turtle was strange, but she didn't think twice about riding one.

"This is so cool," she said as the giant turtle lumbered slowly down the beach.

"Cool?" Francis asked. "It's actually quite warm today."

Nicholas, Zoe, Katie, and Jacob started to giggle, and their giggles turned into laughter. It didn't take long until they were all laughing hysterically.

"Did I miss something?" Francis asked, clearly confused.

"No," Nicholas said, winking at the girls conspiratorially. "Everything's fine."

The children soon tired of the turtle and left it to play on the beach. They were collecting shells when Francis called them back to the Rock. "Time to go!" he yelled. The children raced down the beach and followed him up the jungle path back to Falconhurst, chatting and laughing the entire time about all the fun they had experienced together.

Up in the tree house, Grandma had set the table and ladled soup into bowls. Freshly baked bread was cut for dipping in the soup.

"This soup is delicious," Katie said, sopping up the last of the soup with a soft piece of bread. "What kind is it?"

"It's turtle soup," Grandma answered. "I'm glad you liked it."

Zoe looked down at the table, trying hard not to laugh. Katie sat stunned. She looked at the piece of bread she was holding. Zoe thought that Katie might be sick for a moment, but then Katie smiled, shrugged her shoulders, and popped the bread with the last remains of the soup into her mouth. What could she say? It was delicious.

Chapter 7

While Jenny and the boys were working on clearing up the lunch mess, Grandma took the girls up to her bedroom.

"While you children were at the beach this morning, Jenny and I gathered some clothes for you to wear at the lagoon." Grandma gestured to the clothes laid out on her bed. Outgrown by the boys, the articles of clothing had been stored in a chest. There were two sets of dark long shorts and tight-fitting tops made out of a canvas-type material. The clothes would allow them to move freely while at the same time being modestly covered.

"Thank you," Zoe said.

"I didn't have time to measure you this morning, but I've been sewing clothes long enough to have an idea of your size," Grandma said, handing the girls the clothes. "Go try them on in your room, and if we need to make any quick adjustments, we can do that right now."

When the girls tried on the clothes, they were not surprised that they fit perfectly. When they showed Grandma, she smiled and nodded. She handed the girls a simple cloth bag to put their other clothes in and then took them back down to the living room.

As they were leaving the tree house, Grandpa, Fritz, and Francis slung rifles over their shoulders. Zoe and Katie had been nervous the day before when they had seen the men carrying the guns, but now they understood they needed the guns to protect the family from dangerous animals like wild boars and jungle cats.

As the family approached the edge of the clearing toward the path that led to the lagoon, Zoe turned around and looked at the tree house one last time. It really was amazing, and she wished her family could see it too. She had taken pictures with her iPhone at the Rock and captured Katie on the giant turtle at the beach, but she didn't have a good picture of the tree house. She asked everyone to stop for a moment and rummaged around in the bag Grandma had given her until she finally found her cell phone. The phone still had no reception, but there was a bit of life left in the battery. She pointed the camera toward the tree house and took a picture.

Zoe took several pictures of the tree house and the gardens and outbuildings. She went into her photo collection and checked her work, quickly scrolling through what she had to make sure the lighting was OK and that nothing was blurry. It had suddenly gone quiet, and she could feel bodies pressed around her, trying to get a glimpse at the images on her phone.

"What is that?" Francis asked, pointing to the phone screen.

Zoe could feel her cheeks getting hot. "I just wanted to take a picture of Falconhurst to show my family."

Francis looked at the image on the phone very carefully. The Robinsons had pictures in their home, but they were made with watercolors or oil paints. He had never seen anything so real and detailed . . . and so small! It was astounding.

"Hey!" Katie said, excitement in her voice. "Let's take a group picture."

"Good idea," Zoe replied. She arranged the Robinsons behind her and then snapped a few quick group selfies. When she checked the photos, she had to stifle a laugh. Katie and Zoe were smiling in their island swimming outfits, and the Robinsons were surrounding them with serious, slightly confused expressions on their faces. The tree house was visible in the distance. "I think that's enough pictures for today," Zoe said, stowing the phone back in her bag.

The group continued on into the jungle. They had been hiking only a few minutes when Fritz called out, "Watch your step up ahead near the bend in the trail. Stay to the right."

"Why?" Zoe asked Nicholas.

"There's a trap in the trail," Nicholas replied.

"A trap?" Katie asked.

"Oh yeah," Zoe nodded, remembering the stories her dad had told her about the Robinsons, "you have traps all over the island to protect against bad people."

Francis was walking behind the younger children and listening thoughtfully to their conversation. "I really can't believe how much your father seems to know about our family," he interjected.

"I know," Zoe said, looking at Francis over her shoulder. "He feels like he has a close connection with your family."

Francis nodded thoughtfully.

"Katie and I were trying to build a tree house when we found the magic tree yesterday," Zoe continued. "But after seeing Falconhurst, I'm going to have my brothers help us build a tree house like yours."

"You have brothers?" Francis asked. "How old are they?"

"Yes," Zoe nodded. "Two. Bryce is eighteen and Alan is seventeen."

Francis nodded thoughtfully. He was twenty-three years old, not much older than Bryce and Alan. He wondered what it would be like to live two hundred years in the future.

A few minutes later the group arrived at the lagoon. The sun was high overhead and sunlight glistened on the water. Everyone was hot from the hike and anxious to cool down with a dip. Grandma and Grandpa found a comfortable spot in the shade while Jenny took Anne to the edge of the water to play in the shallows. Fritz and Francis took Zoe and Nicholas to the cliffs to jump while Katie and Jacob took turns swinging into the water from the rope swing.

The lagoon was just as fun as it had looked the day before when the girls had watched from their hiding spot up the hill. In fact, it was even better. The sun was hot, the water was cool, and there were no crowds to compete with. Robinson Island was an unspoiled paradise.

"Father?" Nicholas asked. "Can we show Zoe and Katie the waterfall?"

"Sure," Fritz replied, smiling. He gave a long sharp whistle that caught Jacob's attention as he pointed to the waterfall and made some hand signals. Zoe had no idea what he was trying to communicate, but Jacob did. She could see him gesturing to Katie when she and Jacob began making their way up toward the waterfall.

"Come on, Zoe, you're really going to like this!" Nicholas launched himself off the large rock they were standing on into the deep water below. Zoe waited a moment until Nicholas swam out of the way and then jumped in after him. They swam together to the shore and met up with Jacob and Katie.

The boys followed a path known only to them through the rocks and boulders right next to a gentle waterfall. One minute the boys were leaning against rocks, and the next minute they seemed to disappear. Katie and Zoe were a little frightened when Nicholas' arm appeared in the space between the waterfall and rocks. Zoe grabbed hold of his hand and was pulled into a hidden cave. She looked around, amazed, as Nicholas helped Katie enter.

"What do you think of our cave?" Jacob asked, excitement shining on his face.

"I've never seen anything like it," Zoe answered.

"Yeah," Katie agreed. "It's like something you only read about in books."

"Just wait until you see this!" Jacob said, shimmying up the flat incline on the cave floor. When his head was touching the roof of the cave, Jacob pushed hard and launched himself down the slick surface of the cave floor and shot out through the waterfall into the deep water of the lagoon below. It was a naturally occurring slide.

"I want to try!" said Katie, scooting her way up the incline and hurling herself down through the waterfall.

The children spent the next couple of hours climbing the rocks and sliding out through the waterfall. The longer they did it, the more adventurous they became and earned quite a few cheers from the adults as they slid out head first, backward, and every other way they could think of.

They might have continued on that way for the rest of the day, but they stopped when Grandpa stood up and whistled them over. It was almost four o'clock. The girls found a secluded spot, where they changed out of their homemade swimming suits and back into their modern clothing. It was time to check the tree.

Chapter 8

The group made the easy hike up to the giant tree. Not sure exactly what time it was, they stood around waiting.

"Do you think it'll appear?" Jacob asked.

"I don't know," Francis answered thoughtfully. The explanation the girls had given as to how they arrived on the island was strange and unbelievable. If it hadn't been for the strange clothes and the phone the girls had shown them, he would never have believed their story. Francis knew from private conversations that the other adults were skeptical too, but they didn't see any harm in returning to the tree.

Zoe and Katie stood holding hands, nervously watching the

tree. The past twenty-four hours had been a lot of fun, but they wanted to go home. The thought that the door might never appear again made Zoe's tummy ache. She did her best to hide her fears though, not wanting to scare Katie.

The group stood waiting quietly for several minutes. Eventually Katie looked up at Zoe, tears forming in her eyes. Zoe smiled at Katie and squeezed her hand, trying to give her comfort.

Grandma walked up behind the girls and put her arms around their shoulders. She was about to pull them away when the stones at the base of the tree began to glow. The Robinsons were stunned. They had never seen anything like this.

"Look!" Nicholas yelled, pointing to the giant tree trunk. The unmistakable door had appeared.

"Yes," Katie shouted, "that's it! That's what happened."

Relief flooded over Zoe. They weren't stuck on Robinson Island. They would be going home soon. They walked up to the door, followed closely by the Robinsons.

Francis was standing next to Zoe at the front of the group. "Put your hand through," Zoe suggested, a knowing smile on her face.

Francis needed very little encouragement. He immediately reached toward the door.

"No, Francis," Grandma called, grabbing hold of the back of his shirt.

Zoe could see how nervous the Robinsons were. She stepped toward the tree and put her hand through the door. Her hand disappeared.

The Robinsons gasped. Fritz grabbed hold of Nicholas and Jacob. The boys had no fear and there was no telling what they might do.

Zoe quickly pulled her hand back out through the door and waved it in front of her. "See?" she reassured them, wiggling her fingers. "It's OK."

Grandpa looked at Zoe's hand and then studied the door in the tree. "So it was true then," he mused.

Katie giggled. "Of course it was true. How else could we have gotten here?"

Francis quickly put his hand through the door and pulled it out. He looked at his hand. Everything felt fine.

Zoe smiled at Francis. "Put your head through and take a look," she encouraged.

Francis smiled back, nodding. He moved closer to the tree and poked his head through the door. Grandma took a deep breath and held it. After a few long moments, Francis pulled his head back through the door. Grandma let her breath out.

"What did you see?" Fritz asked.

"I saw a beautiful green forest, although the trees were much different from the trees we have here."

"Try to describe them," Grandpa encouraged.

"Well," he began, "they looked a lot like the trees Ernest described in England."

"They could be pine trees," Grandpa suggested.

"Actually, they're fir and cedar trees," Zoe said proudly.

"I want to see," Jacob squealed, trying to free himself from his father's firm grasp.

"Hold still, boys," Grandpa advised. "We don't know how much longer the door will be here, and we don't want Zoe and Katie to miss their opportunity to go home."

"I wish you could all come with us," Zoe said, looking at the Robinsons' friendly faces. "My family would love to meet you . . . especially my dad."

An awkward silence fell on the group. The Robinsons were nervous and didn't know what to say. Everyone except Francis.

"I'll go," he said confidently.

Grandma looked at Francis, fear written all over her face.

"Are you sure, son?" Grandpa asked.

"I'm certain," Francis said. "I want to go."

"No," Grandma said. "There's too much we don't know about where Zoe and Katie live, and we don't know enough about this tree."

Grandpa nodded, thinking. "Not this time, Francis," he said. "Right now we need to focus on getting the girls back to their family."

Francis nodded. He was disappointed, but he respected his father and mother and knew they had his best interest in mind.

"Well," Zoe said, breaking the silence, "we'd better get going." She picked up the cloth bag Grandma had given her earlier that day.

"We'll be back," Katie assured them, looking directly at the boys. "And when we do, we'll bring our family with us."

"When you do come back, be sure to whistle three times

when you get to Falconhurst," Fritz instructed.

The girls must have looked confused because Grandpa explained, "Three whistles lets us know you're friendly."

Zoe nodded. Now when she looked at the Robinsons she didn't see strangers, she saw friends.

Grandma stepped forward, pulling Zoe and Katie into a hug. "I hope to see you both again," she whispered.

"Thanks again," the girls said, backing up to the door. With one last wave, they joined hands and walked through the door.

The Robinsons stood in tense silence, waiting for the door to disappear. Suddenly Katie's head popped back through.

"Are you sure you don't want to come with us?" she asked.

The tension broke and the Robinsons burst into laughter.

With a final wave and a smile, Katie disappeared. A few moments later the door began to fade away. The stones on the ground dimmed. The tree was a normal tree again.

Chapter 9

Zoe and Katie stood silently as the door in the tree faded and the stones surrounding the tree slowly dimmed. They might have stood there for quite some time, pondering their wonderful adventure, but the cell phone in the cloth bag at their feet started to buzz.

Zoe fumbled to get the bag open as the phone continued to buzz and vibrate.

Zoe looked at the phone. It was 6:32 p.m. and the date on the phone was the same day they had first stepped through the door on the tree.

"Strange," Zoe mused.

She also noticed multiple missed calls from both Mom and Dad, and the most recent text from Mom didn't look good.

WHERE ARE YOU??!

Zoe opened the phone and tried to respond to the last text to let her parents know that they were safe, but before she could hit Send, the phone died.

Katie watched her sister turn white. "What happened?" she asked. "What's wrong?"

"The phone died," Zoe said, shoving the phone in her back pocket. We have to get home right now!" She grabbed Katie's hand and the girls started running.

The girls burst through the back door into the kitchen, completely out of breath. They expected to see their mom standing in front of the stove finishing dinner, but the kitchen was empty.

"Mom!" Zoe yelled, her chest heaving from their frantic run. "We're home!"

The house was silent.

"Hello?" Katie called. "Is anyone home?"

The girls suddenly heard someone pounding down the stairs. A moment later their mom and dad burst into the room. They looked at the girls, relief flooding their faces. Suddenly their mom started to cry.

"Where have you been?" Dad exclaimed, his relief quickly turning into anger. "We have been worried sick!"

The girls watched their mom crying and felt terrible. They'd never meant to upset her like this.

"She's been trying to reach you two for hours," Dad continued, putting his arm around their mom. "What's the point of you having a phone if you don't answer it?"

"I'm sorry, Mom," Zoe sheepishly said. She had never felt so bad in her entire life. "There was no reception where we were, and when we finally got your texts and messages, the phone died."

"It's true, Dad!" Katie added.

"Where were you?" Dad asked. "You were supposed to be in the woods building a tree house. We've never had trouble getting reception in the woods."

Zoe looked down at her feet. She had been so excited to tell her family about the Robinsons, but now that she was standing in front of them she realized how crazy the whole story sounded. If someone told her they'd found a magic tree that transported them two hundred years back in time to a tropical island inhabited by the famous *Swiss Family Robinson*, she would probably think they were crazy.

Zoe had decided to say nothing when Katie blurted out, "You're never going to believe what happened, Dad!"

Zoe looked at her mother, who had stopped crying and was watching the girls carefully. Zoe knew that look well. Her mother had the ability to tell if they were telling the truth or not just by looking at their faces.

"Please," their mother said, clearing her throat, "tell us what was so important that you couldn't manage to take a moment or two to send me a text letting me know you were all right."

Katie's excitement spilled over, and she began to explain.

"We were in the woods collecting branches for the tree house when I thought I saw a bear. We ran deep into the woods to get away from it, but it turns out it was just a deer and not a bear at all."

Zoe watched her mom looking at Katie while she talked. It was impossible for Zoe to tell what her mom was thinking.

". . . and then the stones around the tree started to glow," Katie continued, her face expressing excitement. "And then a door formed in the trunk of the tree."

Zoe shifted her gaze to her dad. A smile played on his lips as he listened to Katie telling her story, but he was trying not to show it.

". . . we touched the door and our hand disappeared. I was scared at first, but my hand was fine, so we decided to put our heads through to see what was on the other side. And do you know what we saw?" Katie asked. She didn't wait for an answer. "A jungle."

Zoe looked at her mom again. She looked annoyed.

Katie kept going. She was so excited to tell her parents what had happened that she never stopped to consider how crazy the story sounded.

"So of course we stepped through the door to take a better look, and it was amazing. It was hot and humid and there were monkeys playing in the trees."

"Monkeys?" their dad asked, smiling.

"Yes!" Katie replied, her excitement building. "And when we walked down the hill a little way, we heard people and you'll never guess who we met, Dad. It was the Swiss Family Robinson!"

"OK," their mother said. "I've heard enough. Give me the phone please," she said, looking at the girls, "and then go to your room."

Zoe handed the phone over. She knew better than to argue with her mom, but Katie kept talking. "You've got to believe us," she said, tears filling her eyes.

"Listen to your mother, girls," their Dad advised.

Katie and Zoe quietly left the kitchen and went upstairs to their room. "They don't believe us," Katie said, flopping down on her bed.

"Give them time," Zoe said, sitting on the edge of her bed. "They'll come around eventually." But she wasn't sure she even believed herself.

*****

In the kitchen, Zoe and Katie's mom plugged the phone in. "Well, TJ," she said, rubbing her eyes, "our daughters have your vivid imagination."

TJ chuckled, nodding. "You've got to give them credit though, Bella. It was a pretty good story."

TJ and Bella spent the next several minutes organizing dinner. It would be a simple meal since they'd spent so much time searching the woods for the girls and calling all their friends.

Dinner was almost ready when TJ picked up Zoe's phone. He scrolled through text messages looking for a reasonable explanation of where the girls had been, but there was nothing there to make him worry. He was about to put the phone down when it occurred to him to look at the photos on it. The girls loved taking photos, and it was very likely that they would have taken some wherever they had been.

The first picture TJ saw was the last picture Zoe had taken. It was the group picture of the girls and the Robinson family with the magnificent tree house plainly visible in the background. TJ's surprise turned to shock as he scrolled through the pictures in Zoe's camera. There were pictures of the smithy, views of Falconhurst from the tree house, the Rock, and Katie smiling happily as she sat on the back of a giant turtle. Interspersed throughout all the photos were the people from the group shot, mostly unaware they were being photographed.

TJ was silent as he studied the photos. He had never seen these people before and yet he knew them. He had never seen the tree house before or been on that island and yet he knew everything about them. They were exactly as he had written them in his novel. They were the Swiss Family Robinson.

"Hey, Bella," he said, getting his wife's attention. "Come look at this."

*****

Zoe and Katie had been sitting in their room for thirty minutes or so when their mom and dad knocked softly on their door.

"Come in," Zoe called from her bed.

TJ and Bella came into the room and sat at the foot of each bed. TJ was holding Zoe's phone in his hand. "Your mom and I checked your phone," he said, looking at Zoe. "We saw some pretty interesting pictures that we'd like you to explain."

Zoe looked at her father. She didn't know what he was talking about at first, but then she grinned, suddenly remembering. "You saw them," she said. "I wasn't sure if the pictures would make it back through the tree. We didn't have any reception there or we would have called," she said looking at her mom. "I'm sorry you were so worried about us. I feel really bad about that."

Bella smiled at her daughters, and the girls knew at that moment that everything was going to be all right.

"We have a lot to talk about," TJ said, standing up.

The front door opened and slammed shut below. "It sounds like your brothers are home from practice," Bella said, standing up. "Let's go down to eat, and you can tell us what happened again now that we're all calm."

Katie and Zoe looked at each other, relieved. That sounded like a great idea.

Chapter 10

Dinner the night before had been long and lively. Bryce and Alan were amused as the girls told their story again in great detail while their dad asked a lot of questions. The boys reluctantly acknowledged that the story might be true once Zoe's phone was plugged into the TV and the family studied the pictures from Robinson Island. As unbelievable as the story sounded, there was no other explanation for the pictures.

It was finally decided the entire family would meet at home after school the next day to go find the tree. TJ would text the football coach and let him know that Bryce and Alan would be missing football practice, and Bella would pick the girls up from school and come straight home.

TJ reminded everyone of the plan the next morning over breakfast.

"All I could think about last night was Robinson Island," he said, pouring glasses of orange juice. "I think I only slept two hours."

"Come on, Dad," Bryce said between mouthfuls of toast. "You don't really think there's a magic tree in the woods, do you?"

Katie glared at Bryce. She was about to say something sassy when her father put a hand on her shoulder and smiled.

"I don't know," TJ replied, "but we're going to find out. Don't forget, everyone needs to be home no later than 3:30 p.m. We have a specific time frame to work in and I don't want to be rushed."

The kids nodded. A change in routine felt exciting.

The girls put their dishes in the sink and ran upstairs to brush their teeth. Katie was finishing up and getting ready to leave when Zoe stopped her. "You can't tell anyone about the Robinsons," she warned.

"I know!" Katie said, annoyed. "You already told me that."

Zoe looked at her a moment longer before smiling. "Let's go," she said. "We don't want to be late today."

Bella was waiting downstairs to take the girls to school. The boys had already left. Bryce was eighteen and a senior in high school, and Alan was just a year younger, so they took turns driving to school in the beat-up old car they shared.

When they arrived at school, Bella stopped the girls before

they left the car to remind them that when school ended they needed to hurry to their regular meeting spot as fast as they could. The girls were on pins and needles all day long and had a hard time concentrating on their classes.

The moment they were dismissed at 2:45 p.m., they ran out of school as fast as they could. They piled into the car, breathless. As they drove away ahead of the crowd, Zoe noticed Katie crying.

"What's wrong, Katie?"

Katie looked at Zoe, tears falling from her eyes. "I told Keeley."

"What?" Zoe exclaimed.

"Calm down, Zoe," Bella said. "There's no reason to yell."

Zoe folded her arms and leaned back in her seat.

"Tell us what happened," Bella said calmly.

"Keeley kept asking if we could play today, and I told her that we had some special family plans today, but you know how Keeley is," she cried. "She kept asking me what we were doing, and the less I said, the more she asked."

"That sounds like Keeley," Bella laughed.

"Finally, I just couldn't take it, so I told her," Katie said.

"And what did she think of your story?" Zoe demanded.

"Actually, she laughed," Katie said. "She said that I shouldn't tell stories and that if I didn't want to play then I should just say so."

"See?" Bella said, looking at Zoe. "There's nothing to worry about."

Bella and the girls got home just before Bryce and Alan.

They all found TJ in the house packing a backpack.

"What's all this?" Bella asked.

"I'm not going on a wild adventure without having a few things," TJ answered. His excitement was infectious, and soon the entire family was finding little items to add to the bag. They packed a knife, a flashlight, a flint and steel, a whistle, and a battery to recharge his phone. He also packed a camera, his journal, and a pen.

"Is there anything else you want to take?" he asked the girls.

"I was thinking we should take some gummy bears or something," Katie suggested.

TJ chuckled. "Good idea. Go grab some and throw them in the bag."

"Anything else?" he asked the boys.

"I was thinking I should take some LEGOs," Alan said sarcastically. Zoe shot him a dirty look.

"OK," TJ said, calling his bluff. "Run up to your room and find some."

Alan laughed good-naturedly and ran up to his room. It had been years since he'd played with LEGOs, but he couldn't bring himself to throw them out, so there were bags and buckets of the tiny pieces in the back of his closet.

The backpack was almost full. "Anything else?" TJ asked. "Last chance before I close this up."

"Swimsuits!" Zoe blurted. "We're going to a tropical island, so we'll probably want our swimsuits."

There was one last rush as everyone ran to get their swim clothes.

"OK," TJ said, struggling to close the backpack, "we'd better go. Lead the way, girls."

Zoe led them out of the house, through the backyard, and into the woods. They were having fun laughing and teasing each other as they wove their way through trees and bushes, moving farther and farther into the woods.

When they reached the clearing, Zoe stopped and pointed to the tree. "This is it."

"Wow!" Alan said. "That tree is huge. I can't believe we never found it before."

"Seriously," Bryce agreed. "We know these woods like the back of our hands, and I've never seen it before.

The family gathered around the tree.

"Hey!" Katie yelled. "Here's the bag Grandma Robinson gave us." She picked up the bag and handed it to her mom. Bella opened it up and pulled out the clothes Grandma Robinson had made for the girls to swim in at the lagoon.

"We were in such a hurry to get home yesterday that we forgot all about it," Zoe explained.

TJ checked his watch. It was 4:15 p.m. He studied the tree. If anything was going to happen, it would happen any moment now.

Soon the stones on the ground started to glow.

TJ quietly pulled out his phone and made a note: tree door opens at 4:17 p.m.

As the stones glowed brighter, the door in the tree appeared.

"Whoa!" Bryce breathed.

Zoe and Katie smiled, feeling completely vindicated.

TJ cautiously walked toward the tree with his phone in his hand. When he pressed the button to take a picture, the door in the tree instantly disappeared. "Interesting," he said to himself, making a note of what had just happened.

"Hey, where did the door go?" Zoe asked.

TJ turned off his phone and put it in his back pocket. The door in the tree reappeared.

"It looks like the tree doesn't like technology," Alan suggested. "Just like you, Mom!"

Bella smiled and shook her head at her son.

TJ was studying the tree carefully, oblivious to the chatter going on around him. "This tree must have some sort of intelligence," he mused.

"Are we just going to stand here looking, or are we going to go through?" Bryce asked.

"Yeah," Alan agreed, "let's go!"

Zoe stepped forward. "All you have to do is step through. Like this." Zoe suddenly disappeared.

Bella gasped and lunged forward. TJ held her tight.

Katie jumped through right after Zoe. Alan stepped forward next. He stood in front of the door and thrust his arm through. It disappeared. He pulled his arm back and looked at it. "That's so cool!" he blurted.

"Hurry up, Alan," Bryce said, feeling impatient.

"Yes, we need to move quickly," TJ advised. "We don't know how long this door will last."

That was all the encouragement Alan and Bryce needed. They stepped through, one right after the other.

"All right, honey, you're next," TJ said, placing his arm around his wife's shoulder and guiding her forward. He could tell she was nervous and wanted to make sure they all made it through.

Bella slowly moved toward the tree. She took a deep breath, closed her eyes, and stepped through.

TJ was the only one left. He smiled, adjusted the straps on the backpack, and confidently stepped through the door back in time two centuries to a remote island in the Indian Ocean.

Chapter 11

Katie and Zoe stood watching their family come through the door in the tree. Bryce and Alan were loud and excited, immediately exploring the jungle around them. Their mom stood quietly, obviously stunned at what had just happened, and when their dad stepped confidently through the door, he stood with his eyes closed, smiling.

Zoe walked over to her mom and touched her arm. "Are you OK, Mom?"

Bella shook her head and looked down at Zoe. She took a deep breath and smiled, putting her arm around her daughter. "Oh yes," she said. "I'm fine. In fact," she said, motioning for

Katie to come to her, "I'm better than fine."

"Now do you believe us?" Katie asked, putting her arms around her mom's waist.

Bella laughed and kissed the top of Katie's head. "Of course I believe you."

Bryce and Alan had been doing a little exploring around the tree. "I can't believe this is real," Bryce said, coming back to the group.

"I know," Alan agreed, "this is way better than football practice."

Bella laughed. "It beats doing laundry too!"

"What do you think, Dad?" Zoe asked. TJ was uncommonly quiet as he stood looking at the clear blue ocean and white foam surf in the distance. It was a beautiful sight.

"It looks exactly the same," he said.

"What do you mean?" Alan asked, confused.

"None of this is new to me," TJ explained. "I've seen this island before in my mind." He stood quietly for a moment before continuing. "When I was writing my book I had dreams about this island. Real dreams. It's hard to explain, but I know everything about this place."

Bella smiled. She remembered the detailed conversations they'd had while he was writing. She'd always known that her husband had a vivid imagination. Plus, she'd just stepped through a door in a magic tree, so she didn't doubt his claim.

"Are we going to stand here all day?" Bryce asked.

TJ laughed. "He's right. Lead the way, girls!"

Katie and Zoe led their family down the path to the lagoon. It was still and quiet and very beautiful.

"This is where we were yesterday," Zoe explained.

"Hey, Dad. See that waterfall over there?" Katie said pointing. "Behind it . . ."

". . . is a cave," TJ interrupted. "There's also a natural waterslide that shoots you out through the waterfall and into the lagoon."

Katie was stunned that her dad knew such a specific detail, but Zoe laughed. "You really did see this place in your dreams."

As the family continued down the path away from the lagoon, Zoe instructed them to stay to the side of the trail. "Grandpa Robinson told us that there's a trap in the trail, and we definitely don't want to fall in," she explained.

When the ground began to level out, Zoe knew that they were close to Falconhurst. She explained that they needed to make three loud sounds to let the Robinsons know they were there. TJ opened his bag and pulled out the whistle he had packed. "Will this do?" he asked.

"It's perfect," Zoe smiled.

TJ blew the whistle three times and the family waited.

They had only been waiting a few minutes when Katie started getting impatient. "How long do we have to wait?" she whined.

As if to answer her question, Fritz and Francis seemed to appear out of nowhere, rifles slung over their shoulders. They had heard the whistles in Falconhurst and scouted out the trail, making sure there was no danger, before they greeted their visitors.

"Francis!" Katie called, running forward and nearly knocking him down with a hug.

"Hi, Fritz," Zoe smiled. "It's good to see you again."

Fritz nodded at Zoe. "Yes," he said, "I'm glad to see you again. I see you've brought your family with you."

"I told you we would be back," Katie said. "Where are Nicholas and Jacob?"

"Hold on a minute," TJ said, stepping forward. "First things first. Let me introduce myself. I'm TJ Hoisington." He reached for Fritz's hand and shook it. "This is my wife, Isabelle, and our sons, Bryce and Alan."

"Very nice to meet you all," Fritz replied, shaking everyone's hand. "And this is my brother Francis."

"It's a pleasure to make your acquaintance," Francis said bowing at the waist.

"Where are Nicholas and Jacob?" Katie asked again, barely containing her excitement.

Fritz chuckled. "They're back at Falconhurst. They heard the whistles and wanted to come with us, but I asked them to wait." He motioned down the trail with his arm. "Let's go down before they ambush us on the trail."

The girls ran ahead, anxious to see their friends. They waited at the edge of the clearing for the rest of the group. "Here it is, Mom and Dad!" Zoe said, her arms outstretched.

The group stopped to admire the magnificent tree house.

"Dad," Zoe called out, her eyes shining with excitement, "is this what you imagined?"

"This is exactly what I imagined," TJ replied, gazing upward. "In fact," he said, holding Bella's hand, "this is better."

Fritz whistled as they walked toward the tree house, and moments later Nicholas and Jacob came racing toward them. Grandpa, Grandma, Jenny, and Anne followed.

"Zoe! Katie! You're back!" Nicholas hollered, still running. He would have run right into the girls, but Fritz caught him with his strong arms.

"Thank you, Father," Nicholas gasped, smiling. Jacob was close behind his brother.

"It's good to see you again," Zoe said laughing.

By the time the boys caught their breath, the grown-ups had arrived.

"Good day to you," Grandpa Robinson said, extending his hand to TJ. "Welcome to our home."

"Thank you very much," TJ replied. "I'm TJ, and this is my wife, Isabelle, who goes by Bella."

Bella smiled and shook Grandpa Robinson's hand.

"Of course you know Zoe and Katie," TJ said, "and these are our sons, Bryce and Alan."

"It's good to see you girls again," Grandpa said, smiling at Katie and Zoe. They smiled back, happy to be back on the island with their family. "And it's a pleasure to meet you," Grandpa said, nodding to the boys.

Bryce and Alan were more subdued than usual. It was a lot

to take in all at once.

"I see you've met my sons, Fritz and Francis," Grandpa said, "and I'm William Robinson." Grandpa put his arm around Grandma's shoulders. "This is my wife, Elizabeth, and Fritz's wife, Jenny."

The ladies curtseyed. "We're so glad that you're here," Grandma said, taking Bella's hand. "Like I told Zoe and Katie, Jenny and I are always happy for female companionship here on the island."

Jenny smiled, bouncing the baby girl on her hip. "My daughter, Anne, is only three years old so she doesn't hold very interesting conversations yet."

Bella laughed. She immediately felt comfortable and at ease with the Robinsons. All of the stress and anxiety she'd felt over the past twenty-four hours completely evaporated.

"Don't forget us," Jacob said, tugging on Grandpa's arm.

"No one could forget you," Grandpa laughed, tousling Jacob's hair.

"These are my sons," Fritz said, "Nicholas and Jacob."

The boys beamed. "We thought you'd never come back," Jacob said, looking at Katie and Zoe.

"We've only been gone a day," Zoe laughed.

"Actually," Grandpa said, clearing his throat, "it's been twelve days since you left."

"How is that possible?" Zoe asked.

"Why don't we go back to the house, and we can talk about it there," Grandma suggested.

The group made their way to the giant trees that supported the Robinsons' home. Francis opened the door to the circular staircase and the group made their way up to the living room. When everyone was comfortably seated, they continued the conversation.

"After you left through the door in the tree, Nicholas and Jacob went back to the magic tree every afternoon for a week to be there in case you girls came back to the island," Grandpa explained. "After ten days we decided that it was unlikely you would be returning."

"We were only gone for one day though," Zoe said.

"That's interesting," Francis said. "What time was it when you returned home?"

"That's the strange part," TJ said. "It seems that the girls had only been gone for two hours."

The room was quiet for a moment as they sat contemplating what it all meant.

"Actually, that makes perfect sense," Francis said getting excited. "One day on Robinson Island is equal to two hours in the future."

"How does that make sense?" Alan asked, not quite understanding what Francis was trying to say.

"It's been twelve days since the girls left the island," Francis patiently explained, "but it's only been twenty-four hours in the future."

The adults nodded, but Zoe was still confused. "I still don't get it," she said.

Francis smiled kindly. "It's a little confusing, but basically what I'm saying is that two hours in the future equals one day in the past."

"And if you divide twenty-four hours by two, that equals twelve hours," Alan added. "Twelve days."

"OK," Zoe said, "I get it now. Katie and I have been gone for one day, but for you here on the island we've been gone for twelve days."

"Exactly!" Francis said.

The adults continued talking about the door in the tree and what it all meant, but the kids quickly lost interest. When Jacob started tapping his hand on the floor, Jenny suggested they go find something else to do. They were trying to decide on an activity when Alan remembered the LEGOs he had brought. Alan, Bryce, and Francis moved the kids to the dining room table and dumped the LEGOs out on the table.

"I bet you've never seen anything like this before," Alan said triumphantly.

Nicholas and Jacob were fascinated with the strange little blocks. They looked at the small, colorful blocks curiously. "What are they?" Nicholas asked.

"These are LEGOs," Alan explained, snapping two pieces together. "They're little building blocks."

Intrigued by these strange little objects made of a material they'd never seen before, Nicholas and Jacob watched in eager fascination as Alan quickly built a square box with a roof on top.

"See," he said, holding it up, "it's a house."

Jacob picked up the LEGO creation and turned it around, inspecting it from all angles.

"Go ahead," Alan said, pushing the pieces toward the boys, "try it for yourselves."

"Here, let me show you how," Zoe said. That was all the encouragement the boys needed. They started snapping and unsnapping pieces together as the girls showed them the basics of LEGO building.

"These really are amazing," Francis said, snapping two pieces together. He tossed the parts back into the pile. "Why don't I show you two around," he suggested to Bryce and Alan.

"That sounds like a great idea," Bryce said grinning. He had lost interest in LEGOs years ago and was eager to explore the tree house.

The adults were happily talking when Grandma Robinson noticed the time. "Goodness," she said. "It's getting late. Jenny and I need to start dinner if we want to eat before bedtime." She and Jenny stood up.

Bella stood up too. "I'll help you," she said.

"That's very kind of you, but it's not necessary," Grandma Robinson said kindly.

"I know," Bella said cheerfully, "but I want to help."

"All right then," Jenny said, smiling. "We would appreciate your help."

Katie had never been a big fan of LEGOs, so she offered

to watch little Anne while the women busied themselves in the kitchen. Jenny was grateful for the help.

Grandpa Robinson took TJ down the stairs to tour the Falconhurst grounds. They had just closed the door to the stairwell when Grandma called down to them. "Will you please bring us back some smoked mackerel and tuna when you're done?"

"Yes," Grandpa called back. "How soon do you need it?"

"No hurry," Grandma replied. "Take your time, but don't forget."

Grandpa saluted. "I never disobey the queen. My queen, that is," he smiled with affection.

The men toured the grounds slowly. Grandpa pointed out the blacksmith's shop, the slaughterhouse, and a tidy little cabin built for guests. TJ felt a connection with Grandpa Robinson and enjoyed seeing the home and buildings he had described in his book. The light was starting to fade when they finally made their way to the smokehouse to get the meat Grandma had asked for. The building was expertly constructed to keep creatures big and small from plundering the meat supply. Grandpa unlocked and then opened the secure door, and the rich smell of smoked meat filled the air.

"We had a lot of luck fishing recently," Grandpa explained, putting several large pieces of king mackerel and tuna into a basket. "These should satisfy Grandma."

They carefully relocked the door and made their way back to

the tree house. The sun had gone down and the lanterns in the tree were lit and glowing gently. There was a magical, peaceful feel in the air. TJ looked around and felt like the luckiest man on earth. He had met the Robinsons and had been in their famous tree house. Best of all, he had his family with him on this amazing adventure. What more could a man ask for?

Chapter 12

Katie and Zoe woke up the next morning slightly disoriented. A flock of wild tropical birds seemed to be screaming at each other in the trees—at least, that's what it sounded like to the girls. Realizing they were once again on Robinson Island, they flew out of bed and hurriedly got dressed. They were staying with their parents in the small guest house on the Falconhurst grounds while Bryce and Alan had opted to bunk with Francis in his room. The young men had quickly formed a tight bond, so it was only natural that they stick together.

Katie and Zoe didn't see their parents in the small cabin, but found them sitting on the porch together, quietly observing the beauty around them. The girls sat down next to them. There was no doubt there was a peaceful, dreamlike quality to Robinson Island. There were no noise distractions like in the modern world they were so accustomed to. There were no airplanes overhead, cars racing down nearby highways, or droning of lawnmowers and leaf blowers. Robinson Island was an untouched paradise.

The reverence of the scene was broken when Francis quietly walked into the clearing in front of the guest house, two rabbits slung over his shoulder.

"Good morning," TJ called. "It looks like you've got lunch or dinner there," he said, gesturing to the small animals.

"Yes," Francis smiled, "Mother will be pleased. I trust you slept well?"

"Oh yes," Bella said. "I haven't slept so well in a long time."

Francis nodded, pleased. "Breakfast should be ready shortly. We can go to the house together if you'd like."

The girls jumped up. "Let's go," they yelled, running ahead.

Soon the entire group was seated in the dining room enjoying a large breakfast. The food was simple, but it was delicious and filling.

"What shall we do today?" Grandpa Robinson asked.

"We could go to the beach and see the giant turtles," Katie suggested.

"Like the one you took pictures of?" Bella asked.

Katie nodded and smiled, pleased that her mom remembered.

"Or we could go back to the lagoon," Zoe said.

Bryce and Alan nodded. They wanted to try the waterslide

behind the waterfall.

"I would love to see the Grotto," TJ said.

"What's the Grotto?" Zoe asked, curious.

"It's a cave," Nicholas said. "We stay there when heavy storms come to the island and it's not safe to be in the tree house."

"Really?" Bryce asked. "A cave that you live in?"

"Yes," Fritz answered, chuckling. "When we were first shipwrecked on the island, it was where we lived until we'd finished building the tree house."

"It's really amazing," TJ added. "The floor is carpeted and there are beds, dressers, and even running water."

"That's something I've got to see," Bella said, impressed.

"We don't just use it during storms," Grandpa Robinson said. "We make sure to keep it stocked and ready in case there's ever any danger on the island."

"What kind of danger?" Katie asked.

"Pirates," Jacob whispered loudly.

"When was the last time you had pirates here?" Bryce asked.

"It's been a long time," Grandpa Robinson admitted, "but it's a comfort knowing we have the Grotto to shelter in if the need arises."

TJ listened to the conversation quietly, his thoughts far away.

"How about we go to the Grotto and then spend the rest of the day at the lagoon?" Jenny suggested in her quiet way. The younger children cheered.

"That's all we'll have time to do today before the door in the tree appears," Fritz said. "Unless you were planning on staying longer?"

"No," TJ replied regretfully. "We need to go back today."

"Come on, Dad," Zoe pleaded, "can't we stay longer?"

"No, Zoe," Bella said firmly. "I've got work tomorrow and everyone has school, so we need to get home."

"Your mom is right," TJ said. "Plus, if we're gone for too long, people will worry."

Zoe stopped arguing, remembering how her parents had worried when they couldn't find her and Katie. If their family was ever going to stay longer on Robinson Island they would need to let family and friends know they were going away for the weekend so no one would look for them.

"Don't worry though," Bella added. "I'm sure this won't be our last visit."

That was enough for Katie and Zoe. Their mom always followed through with what she said she was going to do.

"Go and gather what you'll need," Grandma Robinson instructed the children. "It shouldn't take us very long to clean up and prepare a picnic lunch to take with us to the lagoon."

Zoe picked up little Anne while Katie went with Nicholas and Jacob up to their room to get their things.

"We brought our bathing suits," Zoe heard Katie say as they were leaving the dining room.

"Why would you wear a suit to bathe in?" Jacob asked.

Zoe started laughing to herself. She wondered how Katie would explain what a bathing suit was. It was sure to be an entertaining conversation.

*****

It was mid-morning by the time the group was ready to go. They headed off into the jungle on the path that would lead them to the Grotto. As they approached their destination, Fritz, who was leading, stopped the group.

"We must be careful approaching the Grotto," Grandpa Robinson warned. "It's a place of safety and defense for us, so we've set traps to ensnare any attackers." Grandpa Robinson led the group off of the main trail onto a narrow, concealed path. If you didn't know the path was there, it would have been very difficult to find.

"I always wondered how you got in and out of the Grotto," TJ confessed to Grandpa Robinson. "It's exciting to experience it for myself."

The Grotto looked a little like a hobbit house to Zoe. A door had been cleverly fitted into the opening of the cave, giving it a surprisingly welcoming look. The inside of the cave was pitch black.

"Hey, Dad," Katie whispered to TJ, "now would be a good time to show the Robinsons your flashlight."

TJ started to reach into his backpack, but then hesitated. Was it wise to show the Robinsons items from the future? They had already shared the LEGOs, but explaining a flashlight and how batteries worked was another matter entirely. Robinson

Island was free from the complications and pollutions of the future. TJ didn't want to spoil that.

Suddenly a light flared and a lantern was lit. TJ made a decision and put his bag back on his shoulders. He would do all he could to protect Robinson Island for the family he cared so much for.

With lanterns lit, the Grotto became visible. Just as TJ had said, there was a carpeted floor, comfortable-looking beds, extensive food stores, and munitions. It was much cooler inside the cave than out in the tropical jungle, but it was dry and inviting.

As the group became more comfortable in the cave, they moved around, exploring. Bella noticed that the walls sparkled like crystals.

"Are those crystals on the wall?" she asked.

"No," Grandma Robinson replied. "It's salt rock."

Fascinated, Bella continued to explore. She found a small trickle of water seeping through the rocks in the wall. This must be the running water TJ was talking about, she thought. The water gathered in a stone basin and the overflow ran down a chiseled gully to the wall with the door and disappeared into the vegetation on the outside. Bella took a small cup by the stone basin and sipped the water. It was cold, clear, and tasted vaguely of the minerals in the rocks it had traveled through. It was delicious—better than any of the designer water sold in the trendy health food stores in the future.

"What do you think?" Jenny asked. "Do you think you

could live in a cave like this?"

"Actually, yes," Bella answered. "I think I could. I would probably spend a lot of time outside in the sun during the day, but I could be very comfortable living here."

Jenny smiled, pleased with Bella's praise. "Before the tree house was completed and the family was living mainly at Falconhurst, there was a stove in here too," Jenny explained.

"We vented the smoke outside," Fritz explained. "It all worked rather well."

Bella could hear the nostalgia in his voice. "It must have been a very exciting time," she said, gesturing around the cave. "Those first few years," she clarified, "when you were planning and building your home."

"Yes," Fritz agreed. "Very exciting."

It was almost time to leave when Bella took one last moment to looked around. The Robinsons had so little by the standards of the future, and yet they had more than almost everyone she knew. They had built their home with their hands and had managed to thrive alone on the island. They were hardworking and happy and willing to share what they had with complete strangers. The way Bella saw it, they were rich beyond measure.

Chapter 13

Lunch was served in the Grotto before the group resumed hiking through the jungle to the lagoon. Spirits were high as the children and young men launched themselves off the rope swing, jumped off the high rocks, and rocketed on the slide out from behind the waterfall.

Bella stood with Grandma Robinson, and Jenny in the shallow water keeping a watchful eye on baby Anne. Bella was relaxed and content, a feeling that was hard to capture in her normally busy life. It had been a long time, too long, since she had enjoyed the simple company of women.

TJ and Grandpa Robinson sat on the rocks under the shade

of some nearby trees.

"I have a question for you," TJ began. "When was the last time you saw Ernest on the island?"

"Let me think," Grandpa said, concentrating. "It's been about eight months since we saw him last."

TJ nodded, thinking hard. He knew a lot about the Robinson family and their adventures, and he knew from bits of conversation during their visit that something big and dangerous was going to happen on the island, and soon. His first instinct was to tell the family all about what was going to happen, to warn them and give them a chance to prepare, but he wasn't so sure that was a good idea. He felt a responsibility to protect the family from the future. That was why he had decided against showing the family the flashlight and other modern tools he had brought. Would knowing what was about to happen change the future somehow?

And then another thought came to him. The very fact that he and his family were there had already altered the Robinsons' future. There was no going back. He could try to protect them from future technologies for as long as possible, but he couldn't take the knowledge that his family existed and the reality of the door in the tree away from the Robinsons. Like it or not, the future had arrived on Robinson Island.

TJ took a deep breath. "I'm concerned," he began carefully.

Sensing the seriousness in his tone, Grandpa Robinson turned and gave him his full attention.

"I'm afraid I might have some bad news for you," TJ continued.

Grandpa Robinson nodded his head, a look of determination in his eyes. "Go ahead, TJ. You can tell me".

"Given everything I know about your history, I believe Ernest is on his way back to the island."

"But that's great news," Grandpa said.

"Not exactly," TJ continued. "He has been taken captive by his former ship captain and is being held against his will."

"Captain Charlie?" Grandpa muttered, fire creeping into his eyes.

"Yes," TJ confirmed. "Captain Charlie."

The men sat in silence for a time. Grandpa looked over the lagoon at his family. They had worked so hard to build a home here. They had sacrificed living in society so that they could live the way they wanted to without having to answer to anyone but themselves and God. Grandpa understood the dangers of learning about the future, but he wasn't willing to sacrifice his family or their freedom for abstract theories . . . especially if Ernest was in danger.

Grandpa nodded, determined. "Tell me what you know."

"People know about the treasure," TJ said quietly.

Grandpa's head shot up. How was it possible that TJ knew about the treasure?

"Captain Charlie recruited a small army of men in England, and they're on their way here to take the treasure."

"How much time do we have?" Grandpa asked grimly.

"I'm not exactly sure," TJ said. "I only know the general time frame, but based on how long it's been since Ernest was here last, and knowing that it's a four-month journey by boat from here to England . . . I would say it's a matter of weeks. So much depends on the weather."

"Will Ernest make it through the ordeal?" Grandpa asked, his voice strained.

"Yes," TJ replied, smiling. "Ernest will be fine. In fact, no harm will come to anyone in your family."

Grandpa let out a deep breath as relief flooded his body.

Just then Katie yelled from the highest rock. "Hey, Dad! Watch this!"

TJ watched as Katie jumped without hesitation out over the lagoon, her arms holding her chest tightly and her feet locked together at her ankles. She disappeared under the water for only a few moments before her head broke through the surface, a huge smile on her face.

TJ waved to her. "That was awesome!" he yelled.

A few more moments passed in silence before TJ once again turned to Grandpa Robinson. "If everything in the book is true, and it has been so far, you will be well prepared for what is coming."

Grandpa nodded. If TJ was right, then there was a lot to do to prepare. They needed a plan, and quick.

"I know it's risky to interfere with your affairs here on the island," TJ began, "but I have a plan that I think could work. We will go back through the door today as we've planned," TJ continued, "but I will come back with help."

"What kind of help?" Grandpa asked.

"We live close to a military base and I have some friends who are Marines. I'll tell them what's going on and bring them with me to help you defend the island. It shouldn't be too hard," TJ chuckled. "My buddies are always up for an adventure."

Grandpa took a moment to think about it. It would be twelve days before they would see TJ and his friends again. Not knowing exactly when Captain Charlie and his army would arrive was a problem, but in the twelve days before TJ would return with help, Grandpa, Fritz, and Francis would do all they could to fortify the island and prepare for what was going to come.

"OK," Grandpa agreed. "We would appreciate all the help we can get."

Grandpa and TJ continued talking and refining their plan for the next couple of hours. They were so absorbed in their conversation that they didn't notice the women approaching them.

"What have you guys been discussing?" Bella asked. "You both look so serious."

Grandpa stood up and took Bella's hand. "It is serious, but I'll let TJ fill you in on all the details when you get home. Right now we need to make sure your family makes it to the tree in time for the door."

The next twenty minutes were spent rounding up the kids and heading up the hill to the magic tree.

They were waiting for the door to appear when Francis broke the silence. "Father? Mother? May I go with them through the door?"

"I'm afraid it's simply not possible this time," Grandpa replied. He could see the bond Francis had formed with Bryce and Alan, and he wished he could allow it, but he meant what he said. It simply wasn't possible.

Francis was disappointed, but he accepted his father's word on the matter.

"There will be plenty of time for that later," TJ reassured Francis, "but for now you're needed here on the island."

"What do you mean?" Francis asked.

Just then the door appeared on the tree.

"Your family has a lot to discuss," TJ replied, "but I'll be back here in twelve days."

"You will?" Bella asked, surprised.

TJ laughed. "Obviously we have a lot to talk about too when we get home."

"Or we could just stay a little longer," Zoe suggested.

"Zoe," Bella scolded, "we've already talked about this. We have to go home now. In fact," she said, eyeing the door, "we'd better get going before the door closes."

With a wave and a smile, Zoe and Katie stepped through the door, followed by Bella, Bryce, and Alan.

TJ turned to Grandpa one last time. "Why don't you and the family come through the door and stay with us for a few days?" he suggested. "That way you'll all be protected. When Captain Charlie and his men get here there'll be nobody here for him to hurt."

"Thank you for the offer," Grandpa said. "It sure is tempting, but we've got to think about Ernest. We can't abandon him."

"Of course you're right," TJ answered.

"And either way," Grandpa continued, "this is our home and we will defend it."

"Defend the island from whom?" Grandma asked, concern rising in her voice.

"What's happened to Ernest?" Fritz asked.

"I'll tell you all about it when we get home," Grandpa said.

"The door!" Jacob yelled, pointing to the giant tree. "It's fading!"

TJ didn't hesitate. He jumped through the door only moments before it closed.

Chapter 14

"**D**ad!" Katie shrieked as TJ fell to the ground in front of the tree. "We thought you weren't going to make it back."

TJ laughed nervously as he wiped the dirt off his pants. "I'm fine," he said, but a sick feeling had settled into his stomach. What if he had been caught in the tree? Was that even possible? It was too risky to ever find out. From then on he resolved to always go through the door when it first opened to avoid even the possibility of becoming stuck between times.

TJ looked at Bella, and it was as if she had read his thoughts. "What was so important that you would risk not making it back through the door?" she demanded. "And why were you being so secretive at the lagoon?"

Zoe looked from one parent to the other. She had been having so much fun playing at the lagoon with Jacob and Nicholas that she hadn't noticed anyone else. *What is happening?* she wondered.

TJ looked at his family and sighed. "Let's go home," he said. "We have a lot to talk about."

The walk through the forest was quiet. Everyone knew something was wrong, but nobody dared ask about it until they were home.

When they all finally took their seats at the kitchen table, TJ started to explain. "I was speaking with William . . ."

"You mean Grandpa Robinson?" Katie interrupted.

"Yes," TJ nodded, smiling. "Anyway, we were talking and I believe that the Robinson family is in danger."

Bryce and Alan jumped up from their chairs. "Then why did we leave?" Bryce demanded.

"Boys!" Bella said. "Sit down and let your father speak."

"It's hard to explain, but the island was completely familiar to me," TJ said. "It was as if I had been there before."

"But you haven't been there before," Katie said, confused.

TJ nodded. "That's true, but in a way I had, at least in my imagination."

"Your book," Bella said. "You knew the island through your book."

"Yes," TJ said, grateful that Bella understood. "Everything I described in the book was exactly how the island was, right down to the smallest details."

"Yeah," Alan said, "it was really cool how you totally described the Grotto before we even saw it."

"Exactly!" TJ said, getting excited. "Being on the island and meeting the Robinsons was like a constant feeling of déjà vu."

"What does that mean?" Katie asked.

"Have you ever had the feeling like you've been someplace before, or experienced something, the first time you do it?" Bella asked.

"Yes," Katie said, "it's a really strange feeling."

"That's déjà vu."

"Well, like I was saying," TJ continued, "after talking with William . . . I mean Grandpa Robinson," he said, winking at Katie, "I believe the island will be coming under attack from Captain Charlie and his men very soon."

"How soon?" Bella asked.

"It's hard to say, but I think it will happen within the next two weeks," TJ explained.

"Then why did we leave?" Bryce asked again. "If we go back through the tree tomorrow, twelve days will have passed. We might be too late."

There was tense silence at the table.

TJ cleared his throat. "There is a risk that might happen, but William and I came up with a plan. The Robinsons are going to fortify the island and I'm going to get Bryan, Josh, Lee, and Dave to go back to the island tomorrow and help the Robinsons fight."

"I'm going too," Bryce said.

"Me too," Alan echoed.

TJ shook his head. "I'm sorry boys, but the reason why we came back is so that I can leave you all safely here, away from the danger."

There was a small mutiny as Zoe, Katie, Alan, and Bryce all started arguing and outlining all the reasons they should go back to the island to help the Robinsons. TJ listened quietly, knowing that it was best to let the kids speak before he disappointed them again. Eventually the commotion died down and TJ put his hands in the air.

"I know you all want to help, and I'm grateful for that," he said, "but I just can't justify putting you all in danger."

The kids glared, clearly unhappy. "Now would be a good time for you to back me up on this," TJ said, looking at Bella.

"Sorry," Bella said simply, "but I think you're wrong on this one."

"What?" TJ asked, clearly shocked. "OK. Mom and I need to talk this over."

TJ and Bella left the room and returned fifteen minutes later.

"All right, we've made a decision."

Everyone leaned forward in anticipation. Finally, Bella broke the tension. "We will all be going back to help," she said. "All of us."

Cheers erupted from the kids, and Bryce and Alan high-fived each other.

"We know it's dangerous," Bella explained to the kids, "but

we're a family and we're going to stick together."

"I'm excited, but what if something happens? What if Mom and the girls are harmed?" asked thoughtful Bryce.

"That's a fair question. And we discussed every potential angle. What if we split up and something happens like the door doesn't reopen and we are divided as a family forever?" TJ opined.

"Besides, what if something terrible happens to you, Alan, or Dad? I could never live with myself if something happened to you and I wasn't there to help," Bella added.

TJ nodded. He felt the same way about Bella, but it went against every instinct he had to take his family into a dangerous situation. Besides, TJ knew how this story would end and he had a plan.

Chapter 15

Katie and Zoe thought it would be impossible to sleep after such an exciting day, but in reality, they found it extremely difficult to stay awake long enough to say their prayers.

The next morning the family gathered in the kitchen for breakfast. Zoe, Katie, Bryce, and Alan were going to school, as usual, but TJ and Bella decided to take the day off to prepare for their journey to Robinson Island. After the kids left for school, they spent the morning packing bags with anything they could think of that might help them, and since they had no idea what exactly they would need, the process took longer than expected.

While Zoe wandered through the house contemplating

whether an item would be useful to take, TJ went into the office to call some friends who had served in the military to see if they could help out on Robinson Island. It wasn't easy explaining that their help was needed without giving any specifics, but TJ and Zoe had agreed that it was better for their friends to see the door in the tree for themselves rather than trying to explain it over the phone. The conversations were brief and to the point.

"I need your help with a problem," TJ began.

"What kind of problem?" they asked.

"Actually, I'm not sure," TJ explained. "Some friends of ours are in trouble. Serious trouble, and we're going to go try and help them later today."

"What kind of trouble?" they asked.

"It could be anything from a minor confrontation to an all-out rescue mission," TJ continued.

"That sounds serious," they said. "Can you tell me more?"

"I'm sorry," TJ offered, "that's all I can say for now. I'll be able to explain everything better when we get there."

Each friend was silent as they considered the situation.

"It'll only take a couple of hours," TJ continued.

That did the trick. The friends reasoned that nothing could be quite so bad if it could be resolved in only two hours.

TJ's hopes soared as each friend agreed to help.

"One last thing," TJ said before hanging up. "It would be really helpful if you could pack a bag with battle gear."

"Battle gear?" The surprise in each man's voice was clear.

"Yeah," TJ confirmed, "and wear boots. We'll be doing some

hiking where we're going."

There was a general sense of bewilderment among the friends, but ultimately they all agreed to help, even when TJ asked them not to speak of it to anyone, not even to their families.

It was the mark of their close friendship that they all agreed to meet at TJ's house later that afternoon.

*****

When Bella and the kids got home from school at 3:45 p.m., they found Bryan, Dave, Josh, and Lee gathered in the kitchen talking with TJ. They were dressed in combat clothes and were checking to make sure the bags they'd packed were secure. They had brought rifles that were safely stored in bags, and most importantly, they were wearing boots.

"So, let me get this straight," Lee said, rearranging the binoculars in his combat bag. "You have some friends who you know will be coming under attack, and you would like us to help them defend themselves?"

"Yes," TJ replied. "That's exactly right."

"Why will they be coming under attack?" asked Josh, counting boxes of additional ammunition.

"A very large treasure was found on the family's property and word got out," TJ explained.

The men all stopped their preparations and gave their full attention to TJ. Treasure always had a way of complicating any situation.

"Where are your friends?" Bryan asked. He was a strategic thinker and liked having a plan. "Are they close?"

"They're close," TJ began, "but it's a little complicated."

Bella and the girls smiled.

"Complicated how?" Lee asked.

"Well, we're going to walk there, but the distance between us is immense." TJ explained.

"It's going to blow your mind," Alan interjected.

"That doesn't make any sense," Josh commented, clearly confused.

"You're right," TJ agreed, "it doesn't make any sense at all. I wish I could explain it properly, but it's something you guys are going to need to see for yourselves. Trust me. It will make sense soon enough."

"OK," Dave said cheerfully. "I'm in. I like a good mystery."

Josh and Lee nodded as well.

Bryan took in a deep breath. He didn't like going into a situation without all the information. He was an extreme planner, but as he slowly exhaled he looked at Katie and Zoe. They looked at him with a mixture of trust and anticipation and he couldn't bear to let them down. "OK," he said, "I'll go."

Katie and Zoe whooped and cheered and Alan swung his backpack over his shoulders.

It was only a matter of minutes before they'd be back on Robinson Island.

Chapter 16

It was 4:14 p.m. and everyone was standing around the tree. They had bags slung over their shoulders and weapons in hand. TJ and Bryce were also carrying rifles. When they had all set off into the woods behind the house the men were amused, but when the group stopped in front of the tree their amusement turned into confusion.

"What's going on?" Lee asked. "Where are your friends?"

Katie and Zoe felt a little uncomfortable. It wasn't easy to explain the door in the tree, and even harder to explain traveling back in time.

TJ checked his watch. It was 4:15 p.m. "Our friends live

on an island."

"Yeah, you mentioned that earlier," Lee answered, clearly annoyed. "Clearly there's no island here," he said, gesturing to the forest around them.

It was 4:16 p.m. TJ could see the stones around the tree begin to glow. "Just watch," he said pointing to the ground.

The men stared suspiciously at the glowing stones. At 4:17 p.m., when the door on the trunk of the tree began to form, they took a step back, clearly uneasy.

"What is that?" Dave asked. He was scanning the surrounding woods for anything else out of the ordinary.

"Listen, guys," TJ said. "There was no way for me to explain this. You had to see it for yourselves."

"Seriously though," Josh interjected, "what's going on here?"

"This door will take us to an island in the past," Zoe said stepping forward. She could see that the men were nervous, and she thought it might be easier to understand if a child explained. "Our friends live on that island and they need our help, and we have to hurry before the door closes."

To prove her point, Zoe walked confidently up to the tree and stepped through the door, disappearing from sight.

"What just happened?" Lee yelled, clearly alarmed. "Where's Zoe?"

"She's fine, Lee," Bella said, "but she was right. We need to hurry before the door closes." She took Katie by the hand and walked toward the door. "Follow me, boys," she called to Bryce and Alan. The boys smiled and followed their mother, disappearing through the door.

With his family safely through the door, TJ turned to his friends. "Listen, guys," he began, "you're my friends and you've always been there for me, and I really appreciate that, but if this is too much for you"—he gestured toward the door—"I understand."

The men were silent for moment, processing the situation.

"The thing is," TJ continued, "my family is on the other side of that door and I'm not sure if it's safe for them to be there. A small army will be invading the island, and my friends who live there need our help." He looked each of his friends in the eyes. "I'm not a soldier," he said, "but I'll do whatever I can to help, and we'd all be grateful for your help."

"Who's the family?" asked Dave.

"The Robinsons."

"You mean like the Swiss Family Robinson in your book?" Josh asked.

The men looked at each other, trying to determine what they thought of the situation. A lot didn't make sense, but the one thing none of them could deny was the door in the tree and fact that TJ's family had disappeared through it. That was real.

"We have to act now," TJ said, stepping toward the tree. "The door will close soon,"

Each of the men nodded, and Lee said, "We're in." And without any hesitation they all walked through the door.

Chapter 17

Once everyone was safely through the door on Robinson Island, TJ didn't waste any time. "OK, everyone," he said, "until we know what's happening, we have to assume the island isn't safe."

Just then the door in the tree closed. Bryan, Josh, Lee, and Dave lunged forward, slamming their hands into the tree.

"The door's gone!" Bryan yelled, shocked.

"Don't worry," Zoe said, "it will open again in twenty-four hours."

"Twenty-four hours?" Bryan asked. "How will I ever explain this to my wife? She's expecting me home tonight. Besides," he said, turning to TJ, "you told us it would only take two hours."

"Don't worry," TJ reassured him. "When we go through the door tomorrow—assuming everything goes well here—only two hours will have passed in the future."

"Are you sure?" Bryan asked, obviously skeptical.

"This is my third time coming through the door," Zoe explained, "and every time we go back home only two hours have passed."

Bryan nodded, relieved. It was somehow easier to believe Zoe. "OK," he said. Dave, Josh, and Lee were reassured as well.

Bella gathered the girls close to her. "It's really important that we listen to your dad right now," she reminded her children. "Especially you two," she said, looking directly at Bryce and Alan.

"We know, Mom," Bryce said rolling his eyes.

"That's why the guys are here," Alan added, nodding to Dave, Lee, Bryan, and Josh.

"That's right," TJ said firmly. "We're all going to need to be smart and listen if we want to be safe."

While the family was talking, TJ's friends were studying their surroundings. If they were impressed with the beauty of the island, they didn't show it. They had fallen back on their military training and were assessing their surroundings and coming up with a plan.

Lee had the most experience of all the men, so it was only natural that he step forward to lead the group. "How far is it to your friends?" he asked.

"Their home, Falconhurst, is two or three miles away from

here," TJ answered.

"OK," Lee said, explaining the plan. "We'll move down the trail in single file. TJ, you'll take the lead, followed by me and Bryan. Josh will bring up the rear."

Josh nodded. "That sounds good, but what about Bella and the girls?" Josh asked. "Is there someplace safe they can hide until we know what's going on?"

Bella nodded. When she'd insisted that the entire family come to Robinson Island, she'd never intended to put the girls in any danger.

"The waterfall," Bella and TJ said at the same time. They had talked about it the night before and they both agreed that Bella and the girls would hide in the cave behind the waterfall until it was safe to come out.

Katie and Zoe smiled. Hiding in the cave sounded great to them.

"How far away is the cave from where we are now?" Lee asked.

"It's just a couple of minutes down the hill," Bryce explained. "It's not far at all."

"OK, let's head out then," Lee instructed.

"Just to be clear, we'll need to be very careful on the trail," TJ added. "The Robinsons have set traps along the trail."

The men perked up at that bit of information. This was shaping up to be a real adventure.

A few minutes later they reached the lagoon.

Suddenly, Lee raised his hand for everyone to be silent. They could hear the distinct sound of men talking in the distance. The mood suddenly shifted, and everyone felt tense and nervous.

"Quick, get to the waterfall!" Lee whispered.

TJ hugged his girls quickly and pointed them to the path leading to the lagoon. "Remember," he whispered, "don't trust anyone and stay in the cave behind the waterfall until we come for you."

"How will we know it's you?" Katie asked.

"Let's have a secret password," Zoe suggested.

"Good idea," said TJ, smiling. "What should the password be?"

"'Snowball,'" Katie said excitedly. "The password is '*Snowball.*'"

TJ smiled, and nodded.

"Come on, girls," Bella encouraged, a note of panic in her voice. "We've got to hurry."

Bella and the girls scampered over the boulders along the lagoon as they made their way toward the waterfall. TJ and the men watched silently until they disappeared from sight.

Chapter 18

When Bella and the girls were out of sight and TJ was confident that they were safe, he turned and faced Lee, waiting for instructions.

"TJ, I want you, Bryce, and Alan to stay here on that ridge," Lee said, pointing up to a rocky ledge overlooking the lagoon and the trail. "From that position you'll be able to keep watch over the lagoon and trail while the boys and I do some reconnaissance," he finished, nodding to Josh, Dave, and Bryan.

TJ nodded, but Bryce and Alan had a hard time hiding their disappointment. They wanted to be in the middle of the action and felt that keeping watch was a waste of time.

Lee recognized the disappointment on Bryce's and Alan's faces, but this wasn't the time to humor the whims of a couple of teenage boys. The tree on the island was real, and there was still a lot that they didn't know. It was critical that the source of the distant voices be found—and quickly. Reiterating his instructions, Lee nodded toward the ridge and said, "We'll be back to get you as soon as we know what the situation is on the island. Until then, keep alert and out of sight."

As the four men disappeared into the jungle, TJ, Bryce, and Alan positioned themselves on the ridge behind some low bushes. Hidden from view, they were able to keep a clear watch on the lagoon and the trail, just as Lee had asked them to do.

Out in the jungle, Lee, Bryan, Josh, and Dave crouched low to the ground and silently spread out ten feet apart from one another. They moved silently through the jungle, inching ever closer toward the talking men.

Lee stopped and, using hand signals, directed Dave and Bryan to flank the unknown men on either side. Nodding their understanding, Dave and Bryan disappeared into the jungle. Lee then signaled to Josh to hold his position and keep watch near the trail. It would be his job to alert the other men to any additional threats. Josh nodded and walked silently backward, hiding in the jungle brush.

While he was moving into position through the thick foliage of the jungle, a large black snake lowered itself from a branch right in front of Bryan's face. Without making a sound, Bryan pulled a knife from his hip and struck the head of the snake before it had a chance to strike, its lifeless body sliding to the ground with a soft thump.

Bryan looked at Dave, who had paused to watch ten feet away, and gave him a thumbs up.

A few moments later, the men were in position and close enough to hear the conversation of a small group of men who were huddled together.

"Captain Charlie's going to have our heads if we don't get back to the group," one man said.

"That's if they're still alive," another said nervously, shaking. "This island is cursed!"

It was immediately obvious to Lee and the other men that this group was not friendly toward the Robinsons. They were Captain Charlie's men.

Captain Charlie's men had no idea that they were surrounded by Lee, Dave, and Bryan. As they listened to the conversation, Lee noticed one of Charlie's men walking toward the tree Dave was hiding behind. Dave stayed perfectly still as the man walked just past him and stopped. When the man lowered his pants to urinate, Dave reached forward and tapped him on the shoulder. Startled, the man looked up and was about to yell when Dave covered his mouth and put him in a choke hold. He dropped to the ground silently and was completely unconscious in a matter of moments.

It didn't take long for the rest of Captain Charlie's men to notice that their friend had disappeared. Unnerved, they lunged for their rifles, but before they could defend themselves, Lee and

Bryan appeared out of the jungle, weapons drawn and pointed at the men. Captain Charlie's men were stunned and scared. They didn't know what to think of the large men with their strange clothes and guns.

"Step away from your weapons!" Lee commanded in a calm and firm voice. "Now!"

For a moment it looked like Charlie's men would obey, but then, as one, they began to move.

Dave lunged forward and knocked a musket out of one man's hand, then tackled him to the jungle floor, his knee holding him firmly to the ground.

The two remaining men ran frantically up the trail, hoping to escape the strange new warriors, but they had no chance. The first man had made it only a few steps when Bryan hit him in the legs, knocking him to the ground. The last man jumped over his friend and ran as fast as he could up the trail. He thought for a moment that he was safe, as the distance between him and the strange men increased, but was sorely disappointed when Josh leaped out of the jungle and tackled him to the ground, knocking the breath out of him.

"Who's your leader?" Lee demanded once the men were gathered together. "How many others are there?"

The men initially refused to speak, but something in the fierce way Lee was looking at them made them realize that it would be best to cooperate.

"It's just us," one of the men grumbled. "We got separated from the others, and we haven't seen anyone for two days."

Lee interrogated the men further, and when he was convinced there was no more information he could learn from them, they bound Captain Charlie's men's hands and feet together with zip ties and gagged their mouths with bandanas. Lee didn't want to hurt them, but he also had to make sure that they wouldn't escape and cause any more trouble on the island.

Lee and the others continued their reconnaissance of the area to ensure that there weren't any more of Captain Charlie's men wandering around. Unfortunately, back at the lagoon, TJ and the boys were about to have their own battle.

Chapter 19

Sitting quietly in the cave, Bella and the girls wondered what was happening on the island. It felt like they had been in the dark, damp cave for days, but in reality only two hours had passed.

"Mom, when can we leave?" Katie whined. "I'm getting cold."

Bella smiled and hugged Katie. "I know," she said. "I'm cold too, but we need to be patient. Your dad will come for us as soon as it's safe."

While her mom was comforting Katie, Zoe crept toward the cave opening.

"Get away from there!" Bella whispered frantically when she noticed what Zoe was doing.

"I just want to take a quick peek," Zoe whispered back, peeking her head out of the cave to look around.

Then suddenly, like a bullet, Zoe shot back into the cave, stumbling over loose rocks and kicking some out of the cave in her hurry to get away from the entrance.

"What's wrong?" Bella asked.

Her heart was pounding and her breathing was ragged, but Zoe managed to put her index finger over her lips, silently telling her mom and sister to be quiet. She turned and crawled quietly over to them and whispered, "I saw a man standing right above the cave."

A feeling a dread filled Bella, but she would never let her daughters see her fear. "Quickly!" she whispered. "Move to the back of the cave." Bella and the girls crawled behind some rocks at the very back of the cave and crowded together for warmth and comfort. It wasn't the best hiding place, but Bella hoped the darkness of the cave would cover them like a blanket.

Above the cave, the man watched the rocks Zoe had kicked fly out through the waterfall. "What was that?" he asked his buddy.

"What?" asked the second man.

"Didn't you see those rocks come flying out of the waterfall?" the first man asked. "And I thought I heard something below us," he said studying the rocks below him. "There's something strange going on here."

*****

Up on the ridge, TJ was watching the situation at the cave unfold through his binoculars. "I think we have a problem, boys," he said, pointing at the lagoon.

"Who do you think they are?" Bryce asked, studying the men.

"I don't recognize them, so they must be Captain Charlie's men," TJ whispered urgently, "but what are they doing out there alone?"

"Maybe they're deserters," Alan offered.

"Or they got separated from the others," TJ speculated. "Whoever they are, and whatever their reason is for being there, we need to take them out before they find your mom and the girls. We need to get down there quickly."

"Why don't you fire the gun and scare them away?" Alan suggested.

"No," TJ replied. "If there are others close by, we don't want to alert them to our presence here."

TJ, Bryce, and Alan grabbed their bags and moved quickly down toward the lagoon, being careful to keep out of sight of Captain Charlie's men.

"I have an idea," Alan said as they reached the edge of the lagoon. "We can distract them with my drone so they won't see us coming."

"You brought your drone?" asked TJ, surprised.

"Of course I did," Alan grinned.

TJ nodded, thinking. "OK," he said after a few moments, "here's what we're going to do. Bryce and I will approach the men from inside the tree line over there." He pointed to the jungle at the edge of the lagoon. "Alan, I want you to use the drone to draw their attention away from where we are so we can get close enough to take them out."

"It's a good plan, Dad," Alan said, "but it should be me and Bryce taking those guys out." Alan could see that TJ was about to disagree with him, so he quickly added, "Bryce and I are younger and can move a lot faster."

"Sorry, Dad," Bryce said, agreeing with Alan, "but you know it's true. Alan and I can get there a lot faster than you can."

TJ was going to protest, but he knew the boys were right, and they were running out of time.

"OK," he agreed reluctantly. "I'll work the drone." Alan and Bryce looked at each other and grinned. This was their chance to prove themselves. "Get going, and be careful," TJ said, bringing them back to reality. "There's no time to lose."

Bryce and Alan nodded once to their dad and moved quickly into the jungle at the edge of the lagoon. TJ found a place where he was covered by the foliage but could still see the men by the waterfall. He pulled Alan's drone from the bag and turned it on. It hummed to life as he guided it by remote into the sky.

The drone was airborne and racing over the blue lagoon toward the two men, who were still inspecting the area around the waterfall.

"I think I found something!" one man exclaimed as he

climbed down, poking his head into the cave opening.

"Do you see anything?" the second man asked.

"No. Nothing."

Distracting the man from entering the cave, TJ sent the drone flying low, directly over both men's heads.

The men dropped, covering their heads. "What was that?" one of them yelled.

Inside the cave, the girls heard the sound of the drone and recognized it instantly. "That's Alan's drone," Katie whispered, a smile spreading across her face.

Bella was relieved to know that help was on the way.

Captain Charlie's men had just stood up when TJ sent the drone flying back toward them. This time, as the drone whizzed by, one of the men lifted his rifle and shot at it.

The bullet missed the drone, but the sound of the ignited gunpowder thundered across the lagoon and the surrounding area. Captain Charlie's men stood frozen as the drone hovered over their heads, just out of reach.

Bryce and Alan took advantage of the confusion to burst from of the tree line and rush the two men from behind. The first man had already fired his musket, so it was useless. Alan grabbed the smoking weapon from him and knocked its owner down with it. As the second man raised his musket, Bryce grabbed it by the muzzle and swung it like a bat into the lagoon. The man put his hands in the air, surrendering, when Bryce turned to face him again.

TJ landed the drone on a rock near the waterfall and then

took off running toward the scene. He stopped suddenly and dove behind a boulder when he saw movement at the edge of the jungle close to the waterfall. He didn't notice he was holding his breath until he saw Lee, Dave, Bryan, and Josh emerge from the jungle onto the trail. Letting his breath out all at once, he stood and whistled to his good friends and gestured firmly to where Bryce and Alan were subduing Captain Charlie's men.

Lee and the rest of TJ's friends ran to help Bryce and Alan. They moved Charlie's men to the edge of the jungle where they could be seen easily and bound them with zip ties, just like they had the other group of lost men. Lee started questioning the men while the others, including Bryce and Alan, searched the surrounding jungle to be sure there weren't any more enemies hiding in the jungle meaning to do them harm.

TJ reached the site but ran past Lee to the waterfall. He called, "Snowball!" at the mouth of the cave before he dared go in. Bella was a kind and gentle woman, but TJ knew she would defend their daughter fiercely if she had to. Slowly entering the cave, he called "Snowball!" once again.

"TJ?" Bella asked from the back recesses of the cavern.

"Yes, it's me," TJ said. "It's safe now. You can come out."

Katie and Zoe jumped up and rushed to their dad. TJ caught them in a firm hug and kissed the tops of their heads. "Everything's going to be all right," he murmured. "Bella," TJ called.

Bella crawled out from behind the rocks and moved forward until she could stand. "We heard a gun fire," she said. "Are the boys . . . ?"

The boys are fine," TJ quickly assured her. "In fact, they're better than fine. They were fantastic."

Bella stumbled forward into TJ's arms. "I was so worried," she whispered.

"I knew you'd protect us," Katie said wrapping her arms around both of her parents.

"Yeah," Zoe added. "As soon as I heard Alan's drone, I knew everything was going to be OK."

"And you were right." TJ laughed. "Let's go out and let the others know you're all right."

TJ led Bella and the girls out of the cave and into the bright sunshine. The light was very bright and it took a several moments for their eyes to adjust, but when they did, Katie and Zoe saw Lee standing over two men who were tied up not very far from where they were standing. Then, like magic, Alan and Bryce materialized out of the jungle, followed by Dave and Bryan. Josh was the last to arrive, and he gave the all clear. The immediate threat from Captain Charlie's men had passed. Would there be more?

TJ led Bella and the girls away from the waterfall, past the captured men, and into the jungle, where they could not be seen from the lagoon. The safety of the jungle covered them like a blanket. TJ's friends gathered around, circling them. Bella stopped shaking. She knew she was safe.

"What did those two have to say?" Dave asked, gesturing toward the bound men sitting ten feet away from them.

"Not much," Lee reported. "They say they were separated from the main group a couple of days ago."

"Just like the other group," Bryan said.

"What other group?" TJ asked. "Were they the ones we heard talking earlier?"

"Yes," Lee explained. "There were four of them. They were separated from the main group as well, but they did say that it's been quiet on the island since yesterday."

"They were convinced that the island is alive and possessed," Josh chuckled.

"In a way it is," TJ explained. "The Robinsons set traps and snares to slow invaders down."

"Well, they did a good job," Bryan laughed. "I've never seen men so afraid before."

After a lengthy discussion, the group decided it was better to stay together. There was safety in numbers, and Bella wasn't interested in staying in the cave with the girls any longer. Whatever dangers remained, they would all face them together.

They cut the zip ties on the two men's legs and led the captives down the trail to their four comrades. They then resecured them with zip ties and gagged them just like the others.

With the captives subdued, the group decided to make their way down the trail to Falconhurst. They moved slowly, paying close attention to their surroundings watching for any new threats, but the jungle was silent.

Chapter 20

The hike down the mountain was uneventful. As they approached Falconhurst, they heard the distinct sound of people walking up the trail.

Bryan put his arm up, stopping the group and motioning for them to crouch down. They waited in tense silence for a few moments until TJ recognized Francis and Nicholas coming toward them.

TJ whistled three times, signaling to Francis and Nicholas that friends were approaching. Francis raised his musket momentarily, but quickly lowered it when TJ stood up.

"Francis, Nicholas," TJ called out. "It's me."

"And Katie!" Katie yelled, jumping up.

As if on cue, everyone began standing up.

Francis and Nicholas smiled and hurried up the path to meet them.

"It's good to see you," Bella said, embracing Francis.

"It's great to see you too," Francis laughed.

Katie and Zoe ran up to Nicholas, who was standing behind Francis. He was happy to see his friends but was holding back because of the men he didn't recognize in their group.

TJ recognized the problem right away. "Nicholas," he said, putting his hand on the young boy's shoulder, "we brought some friends with us."

Francis and Nicholas turned and faced the group.

"This is Lee," TJ said as Lee stepped forward to shake Francis's hand.

"Pleased to meet you, sir," Francis said.

Dave, Bryan, and Josh each came forward and shook hands as TJ introduced them.

"Thank you for coming to help our family," Francis said. "We appreciate it very much."

With the introductions over, TJ asked the one question he really wanted to know. "Is everyone OK?"

"Yes." Francis smiled, reassuring them. "Everyone is fine."

"That's not true," Nicholas cried. "Sunshine is dead!"

Francis put his arm around Nicholas. "Sunshine was our family dog," Francis explained.

"One of Captain Charlie's men shot her," Nicholas cried, struggling to keep the tears out of his eyes.

"That's terrible!" Zoe said.

"Yes, it's been really hard on the kids," Francis explained.

Everyone stood silently for a moment while Nicholas wiped his eyes.

"We do have some good news though," Francis said, breaking the silence. "Do you want to tell them?" he asked Nicholas.

Nicholas' face brightened. "Uncle Ernest and his fiancée Elizabeth are here. I can't wait for you to meet them."

The Hoisingtons smiled. They all knew about Ernest and Elizabeth who came over from England because of TJ's book.

"We look forward to meeting them," Bella smiled.

"And the battle?" TJ asked. "When did it end?"

"Two days ago," Francis answered. "It happened just like you said it would. Thanks to you we had plenty of time to prepare and come up with a plan."

"That's what we thought," TJ said.

"We came across a couple of groups of Charlie's men on the way here," Lee explained.

"You did?" Francis asked, concerned. "We thought all of Captain Charlie's men were either dead or captured. Where are they now?"

"We left them tied up near the lagoon," answered TJ.

"We need to tell Grandpa right away," Francis said, clearly concerned.

After some discussion, it was agreed that Francis and Nicholas would return to Falconhurst and retrieve appropriate clothes for everyone. There were a lot of extra people on the island, primarily the Royal Navy officers, and it would raise too many questions if they all walked into camp dressed in modern clothes, not to mention the camouflage combat clothes Josh, Bryan, Dave, and Lee were wearing.

It took less than half an hour for Francis and Nicholas to return. "Here are the clothes Mother and Grandma set aside for you," Francis explained, handing a large burlap sack to Bella. "It took us a little longer because we had to find additional clothing for everybody else as well," Francis said, looking at Lee and the other men.

Bella sorted through the clothes and handed them out. There were homespun pants and shirts for the men, and dresses for Bella and the girls. The clothes were simple, but the cloth was expertly made and felt soft and comfortable against their skin. There were even soft leather moccasins for everyone to wear.

When they were all dressed, Bella instructed everyone to put their modern clothes in their backpacks. With that accomplished, they hid their modern gear—along with their backpacks—behind a large boulder a little distance off the trail. With so many other people on the island, it was more important than ever to keep their true identities—and the door in the tree—a secret.

As the group began walking toward Falconhurst, the tension from earlier vanished and everyone was happy and talkative. TJ took the opportunity to finally explain to Bryan, Lee, Dave, and Josh who the Robinson family was and how Katie and Zoe had discovered the magic tree.

Josh listened carefully, and when TJ finished, he finally spoke. "I've seen a lot of crazy stuff, but this is probably the strangest thing I've ever been involved with."

"I feel the same way," TJ laughed.

"The thing that's really amazing to me," Josh continued, "is how everything you wrote about is actually happening to the Robinsons."

"I don't really understand that either," TJ admitted. "It's hard to know if I was able to see into the past or if what I wrote is somehow affecting their lives in the past."

"You should really figure that out," Lee advised, "and soon. Especially if you plan on writing another book."

Everyone laughed.

The jungle thinned as they approached Falconhurst. Francis stopped the group and had them gather close together. "A perimeter has been set around Falconhurst," he explained. "The Royal Navy officers are keeping guard, so before we go down, you need to know the story Father will tell to explain who you are and why you're here."

"Dad, why is the Royal Navy here?" Katie asked.

"When word got out that Captain Charlie had a plan to sail from England and attack the Robinsons, the Royal Navy was summoned to help protect the Robinsons," TJ explained.

"The only problem is they arrived a day too late," Alan added, having read *Return to Robinson Island*—proudly emphasizing that the Robinsons had been able to defend against Captain Charlie's army on their own.

"So what about the story Grandpa is going to share?" Bryce interrupted. "This should be interesting."

Nicholas grinned. "Grandpa will tell everyone you're friends from America."

"Well, that's true," Zoe said brightly.

"And your ship is docked on the back side of the island," Francis continued. "We didn't know you were coming, so having you here is a surprise."

TJ laughed. "I think we can manage that." He admired Grandpa's cleverness. The best stories are almost always based on some element of truth.

"Are you ready?" Nicholas asked eagerly.

Bella looked around the group. They looked slightly out of place with their modern haircuts and modern accents, but there were no other physical indications of who they really were or where they had come from. They were as prepared as they would ever be.

"Ready," she said confidently, "let's go."

Chapter 21

As the group made their way past the posted sentries, Katie and Zoe were amazed by the transformation at Falconhurst. Tents were pitched throughout the settlement for the Royal Navy officers. The officers were moving around in small groups, and a constant banging and clattering was coming from the blacksmith's shop as sailors fashioned the tools and hardware needed to repair the ship. On the edge of the settlement, the women oversaw the laundering of the vast amounts of clothing that needed to be washed and mended. The rest of the Robinson family was busy directing various projects. All the activity had transformed Falconhurst from a quiet homestead into a busy little settlement.

"What do you think?" TJ asked his friends.

"This really is amazing," Dave said, studying the tree house across the clearing. Since retiring from the military, he had been working as a construction foreman and loved to build things in the workshop at his house. "I bet they built the tree house using the same techniques shipwrights do to build ships. That way the structures can handle the movement from the trees without breaking apart."

"Huh," TJ grunted, looking at the tree house with new eyes. "I bet you're right."

"You're going to love it here," Katie smiled, taking hold of Dave's hand.

"Just wait till you see the beach," Zoe added.

"The beach is beautiful," Bella agreed.

Lee smiled. "I'd love to go back up to that lagoon and take a look around," Lee said.

"The lagoon is awesome!" Bryce agreed.

Bryce and Alan spent the next few minutes entertaining the group with stories of their adventures from their last visit to the lagoon. Katie and Zoe added details every now and then whenever they could manage to get a word in. The group was laughing and talking when the Robinson family made their way toward where the Hoisingtons were standing.

"William," TJ said, shaking Grandpa Robinson's hand, "it's so nice to see you again."

"Welcome back," Grandpa Robinson said, smiling.

"I'm sorry we didn't make it in time to help."

"Don't you worry about that. Everyone is safe, just like you said," Grandpa acknowledged. "And knowing what was coming was a major advantage to us, and I thank you for that."

TJ nodded and smiled. He may not have been able to fight for his friends, but he was glad that his knowledge of what was coming had been useful.

Bella hugged Grandma Robinson and thanked them for the clothes and shoes.

Grandma chuckled. "Well, we couldn't have you running around the island in your strange clothing," she said. "It would raise too many questions with all the people visiting us at the moment."

Bryan, Josh, Dave, and Lee were introduced to the family, and they slowly made their way through the establishment to the tree house.

"I was hoping to get a tour," Dave said to Fritz, motioning to the structures in the tree. "I'm a builder, and I'd love to know how you managed to construct such a magnificent structure."

Fritz smiled. He had helped build the tree house alongside his father and brothers years ago, and it was a great source of pride for him. "I would be happy to give you a tour."

Lee, Bryan, and Josh were interested in all of the outbuildings and how the Robinsons managed to support themselves with very little assistance from the outside world, so when Francis offered to give them a tour, they eagerly accepted.

Nicholas and Jacob were telling Katie and Zoe all about the ship anchored in the bay when Bryce and Alan suggested they go and see it for themselves. The parents all agreed to the plan, and they happily set off.

When they finally made it up into the tree house sitting room, it was just Grandma and Grandpa Robinson, TJ, and Bella. Grandpa was explaining to TJ how they had prepared the island for the attack when they were interrupted.

"Jenny! Little Anne!" Bella exclaimed, jumping to her feet. "It's so lovely to see you again." Bella hugged Jenny and kissed little Anne on her cheek.

A young man and woman entered the room behind Jenny and Anne. Grandpa stood. "TJ, this is our son Ernest and his fiancée, Miss Elizabeth Cole."

TJ stood and shook Ernest's hand. It was a special treat for TJ to meet Ernest, as the Robinsons second son wasn't able to make the long and difficult journey from England to Robinson Island often. "It's a particular pleasure to meet you," TJ said. "It's nice to see you doing so well after your ordeal on Captain Charlie's ship." Ernest had been held captive on Captain Charlie's ship for ransom for the many months it took to get to Robinson Island. Although he looked thin and a little worse for wear, there was a twinkle in his eyes and energy emanating from him.

Elizabeth, on the other hand, radiated beauty. She had left her family in England and hid on Sir Montrose's ship to go after Captain Charlie, hoping to see Ernest again. To everyone's surprise life onboard the ship had agreed with Elizabeth, and she had become even more lovely than Ernest had remembered her in England.

Elizabeth smiled and curtsied to the group. "I'm very pleased to meet you all," she said.

The last person to enter the room was a distinguished older gentleman with white hair who radiated confidence. Sir Montrose was Jenny's grandpa and the adopted grandpa to the entire Robinson family. He was an English aristocrat and had achieved great wealth as a merchant and owned numerous ships. It was his fastest ship the Royal Navy used to pursue Captain Charlie. Despite is wealth, Sir Montrose remained a humble and kind man and was deeply loved by the Robinsons.

"Can you guess who this is?" Grandpa whispered to TJ.

TJ smiled. "Sir Montrose," he said, stepping forward to shake his hand, "it's an honor to meet you."

Montrose smiled and shook TJ's hand. "Have we met before?" he asked.

"No, not officially," TJ said.

"These are our good friends from America," Grandpa quickly interjected, "Mr. and Mrs. Hoisington."

"From America, you said?" Montrose asked, surprised.

"Yes, well," Grandma said firmly, "we'll explain it all tonight when we have a bit more privacy."

"Yes," Grandpa agreed. "It's a story you won't want to miss."

*****

The next few hours were spent visiting and preparing for dinner. The Royal Navy officers had cooks to prepare their meals, so dinner at the tree house was reserved for family and close friends.

Meanwhile, a contingent of Royal Navy officers were sent back to the lagoon to retrieve Captain Charlie's deserters.

As the Robinsons, the Hoisingtons, TJ's friends, and Sir Montrose sat down to eat dinner, they chatted excitedly about all they had seen. Dave was impressed and inspired by the workmanship the Robinsons had used in building not only the tree house but the other buildings as well. He planned to use many of the techniques he had observed in future projects.

Lee, Bryan, and Josh were equally impressed with their tour of Falconhurst. They were amazed by how the Robinsons had devised so many systems and methods to live off the land. The Robinsons didn't merely survive on the island, they thrived.

When Bryce and Alan returned from the bay with the younger children, they talked over each other in their excitement to share what they had seen.

"Please," Fritz laughed, "speak one at a time so we can understand what you're saying."

The children stopped talking and Alan began speaking. "We went down to the bay to check things out, and Captain Briggs invited us to take a tour of his ship."

"Some sailors rowed us out on a boat, and we climbed a rope up to the deck," Katie quickly added.

"That sounds exciting," TJ said, a little disappointed he hadn't been with them.

"It was so cool," Zoe answered.

"Captain Briggs took us to the bow of the ship and showed us the wheel they use to steer," Katie said.

"It's not a wheel," Jacob corrected, "it's called the helm."

Katie scrunched her face up at Jacob, making the adults in the room laugh.

"Anyway," Zoe said, "we saw the galley, the captain's rooms . . ."

"That's where the captain lives," Katie interjected.

Zoe rolled her eyes. "We held the instruments they use to navigate and even tried to climb the main mast."

"We didn't get very far up," Bryce admitted with a laugh.

"The best part was going down to the brig," Nicholas said.

"You went to the brig?" said Ernest, surprised.

"What's a brig?" Bella asked.

"It's the jail on the ship," Ernest explained.

Bella was shocked. "I'm not sure that was a good idea," she said. "Was anyone in there?"

"Oh yes!" Jacob exclaimed. "There were a bunch of Captain Charlie's men in there."

"Don't worry though, Mom," Bryce quickly added. "Alan and I were there the whole time, and there were a bunch of men from the Royal Navy guarding them."

Bella shook her head disapprovingly. "Well, I don't want you going back there without a parent," Bella said.

"I'll have a talk with Captain Briggs later," Sir Montrose assured the women. "The children will not be visiting the brig again, Mrs. Hoisington, you have my word on that."

"Thank you, Sir Montrose," Bella said, giving her children a stern look. "I appreciate that."

As the conversations wound down, the question of where the Hoisingtons and their friends would stay was answered.

"I thought that perhaps you would be most comfortable at the Grotto," Grandpa ventured. "It's removed from the crowds here, and I thought it would be the perfect place to have important conversations where we won't be overheard."

"That would be lovely," Bella said. "We appreciate your generous hospitality."

"What's the Grotto?" Josh whispered to Zoe.

"It's a house in a cave," she whispered back, "like a hobbit hole."

When the dinner mess was cleaned up, the large group made their way through the jungle to the Grotto. It was dark, but the path was clear, and they carried lanterns to light the way.

As they approached the door to the Grotto, Lee immediately understood why Grandpa Robinson had chosen to bring them there. With only one door leading into the cave, there was no way anyone could eavesdrop on their conversation, and it was crucial that the door in the tree remained a secret.

Inside the Grotto, the lamplight sparkled off the salt rock in the walls and ceiling, giving the room a magical feel. As Grandma lit a fire in the stove to warm the room, Jenny laid the sleeping Anne on a cot. The rest of the group arranged chairs and pillows in a circle. It was going to be a long night of exciting conversation.

Chapter 22

The conversation in the Grotto that night was lively and lengthy. Sir Montrose, Ernest, and Elizabeth had been unsure what to believe at first, but as the story unfolded and TJ was able to give details that no one could have known, they were all eventually convinced. The children had vowed to stay awake all night, but as the evening wore on, they fell asleep on pillows throughout the large room. It was early morning before the last of the adults finally went to sleep.

It was nearly noon when people began waking up. Grandma, Grandpa, and Fritz had left early to attend to the other visitors on the island, but the rest of the group had slept late. When they finally woke up, it was to the savory smell of bacon. Jenny had prepared a late morning feast.

"This is the best brunch I've ever had," Bryce said, his mouth full of food.

Bella grimaced. "Please, son," she chided, "chew with your mouth closed."

Bryce swallowed and loudly gulped down a cup of goat milk. "Sorry, Mom," he grinned.

Bella shook her head. It was hard to reason with boys when food was involved.

"What is a brunch?" Jenny asked.

"It's a late breakfast," Bryce said between mouthfuls. "It's between breakfast and lunch, so it's called brunch."

"How interesting," Jenny mused. Life in the future seemed so different than life here on Robinson Island.

After a lengthy discussion the night before, it had been decided that Bryan, Lee, and Josh would leave through the door in the tree later that day. They had families and work obligations and needed to get home. When they went back through the door in the tree, they would have been gone only two hours, just as TJ had promised. Dave and the entire Hoisington family would stay on the island for two weeks. Dave worked construction and could lend his skills to a special project the Robinsons had. Ernest and Elizabeth were planning to marry soon. The journey to Robinson Island had taken four long months and they were not willing to prolong their engagement another year to travel back to England.

*****

Over the next few days, as the women busied themselves with wedding plans, the men began working on a more sensitive matter. The reason Captain Charlie had kidnapped Ernest was that it was rumored that treasure had been discovered on Robinson Island. Captain Charlie and his men had risked everything to find and steal the treasure, and they'd almost succeeded. TJ's warning had given the Robinsons a tremendous advantage in their efforts to fortify and protect the island, but it was the timely appearance of Baraourou warriors, natives from a nearby island, that sealed the victory for the Robinsons.

"I wish I could have seen the warriors," Zoe said as the children retold the story to one another over the next few days.

"They look fearsome at first," Jacob explained, "but when you get to know them, they're really quite nice."

"It's too bad they didn't stay longer," said Katie.

Jacob nodded, agreeing with Katie. "They usually stay for a while, but when they found out what had been happening here, they decided they should get back to their island to protect their own tribe."

"I can't believe we just barely missed them," Katie whined.

The Baraourous had left the morning of the day the Hoisingtons arrived on Robinson Island. They had missed them by ten hours.

A year earlier, Sir Montrose had taken a few coins to England to make discreet inquiries as to the possible origin of the vast treasure trove. He'd learned from several trusted sources that the coins likely dated to 1556 and were of Spanish origin. The monarchy the treasure belonged to no longer existed, and since Robinson Island had not yet been claimed as territory of any sovereign nation, the treasure belonged to the Robinson family. During the battle, Captain Charlie and his men had managed to retrieve the treasure from a remote cave in the mountain and transported it down the slope before they were defeated. The treasure that had been carefully hidden for hundreds of years had been left sitting in the middle of the forest in five large, rotted wooden chests.

The Robinsons needed people they could trust to help them build new chests to store the treasure in and come up with a plan for where to hide it. Relying on Dave and the Hoisingtons was ideal because they had no ties to anyone, or any countries, in the past. If the Robinsons relied on the soldiers or sailors for help, word of the treasure would spread again, putting the family in continual risk.

The men went about their work stealthily. The children occasionally saw them come and go, and Dave spent several days building a number of sturdy wood boxes, but other than that, their movements were a complete mystery. Not that the children cared very much. They happily spent most of their free time down at the beach. The sailors on Sir Montrose's ship were amused by the children and were happy to let them tag along as they finished repairs to the ship and worked to restock the supplies they would need for their four-month return journey to England.

It was a fun, carefree time for Katie and Zoe. They'd assumed they would get bored on the island after a few days, but between wedding preparations, the mysterious comings and goings of the men, and general fun and mayhem, there was always something happening to keep them occupied. In fact, they were having such a good time that it was a shock when Bella announced that they would be heading home the next day.

"We're leaving tomorrow?" Zoe asked.

"Yes," Bella answered. "We've been gone for one full day in the future, and we can't risk staying away any longer."

"Why not?" Katie cried, tears streaming down her face.

Bella smiled and hugged Katie. "We didn't tell anyone that we would be gone," she explained. "We can come up with an excuse for being gone for one day, but anything longer and people will start to worry."

"Do you think Nanny and Papa are worried?" Katie asked, suddenly concerned.

"No," she answered calmly. "Your dad and I asked Bryan to call and tell them that we surprised you kids with a fun overnight trip and will be out of cell service."

Katie suddenly pulled out of Bella's arms, a look of panic on her face. "Who's taking care of Snowball?"

"Snowball is fine," Bella explained. "I made sure to put out plenty of cat food before we left."

Katie smiled. She could always rely on her parents to take

care of everything.

"I'm just not sure how we're going to explain how tan we've all become," Bella said laughing.

Zoe looked at her arms and legs. They had become several shades darker over the two weeks they'd been on the island. "It doesn't really matter what we say," she chuckled. "No one would believe the truth anyway."

*****

After breakfast on their final day on the island, TJ, Grandpa, Fritz, and Sir Montrose met together. Their plan to secure the treasure had worked perfectly, so they sat at ease knowing that the island was secure and the treasure was well hidden and guarded.

"Sir Montrose and I have been talking," Grandpa said, looking at TJ, "and we both agree that we owe you a debt of gratitude."

"Yes," Sir Montrose agreed, "I shudder to think what might have happened if you hadn't warned the family about Captain Charlie."

"I'm glad I could help," TJ said with feeling, and he meant it. Meeting the Robinson family and spending time on the island had been the greatest adventure of his life.

Grandpa pulled out a large leather bag tied shut with a strong cord and placed it heavily on the table. He untied the cord and opened the bag. It was full of Spanish gold coins. "We want you to have this," Grandpa said, pushing the bag across the table to TJ.

"Oh no," TJ said, putting his hands in the air, "I'm afraid I can't do that."

"Of course you can," Fritz insisted. "There's more treasure on this island than we could ever need, and besides that, what would we spend it on? We get everything we need from the island."

TJ laughed. It was true. He had never met a family so happy and content. They were an inspiration to him and his family. "It just doesn't feel right to take it," he said, looking at the bag.

"We figured you'd say as much," Grandpa said, "but I'm going to have to insist. We are bound together for better or worse, and the treasure is part of that bond."

TJ could see that he would deeply offend the Robinsons if he refused the bag of gold, so after several moments of hesitation, he reluctantly leaned forward and took the bag. It was much heavier than it looked. TJ looked at the men sitting around the table. Sir Montrose, Grandpa, and Fritz were much more than characters in a book to him now; they were his friends. "I'm not sure what to say," he admitted, clearing his throat.

Sir Montrose chuckled, then bellowed, "Don't spend it all in one place!"

Grandpa smiled and nodded at TJ. Sometimes words just weren't enough.

*****

Unfortunately, the time came for them to go home. Stepping back through the tree door into the cool, green forest felt strange. Everything was familiar, but Robinson Island had come to feel just as natural and comforting as home.

"I'm going to miss the Robinsons," Zoe confided to Bella as they walked back to their house.

"Yes," Bella agreed, "we all will."

"Don't worry," TJ said, walking right behind them, the bag of treasure carefully hidden in his backpack. "We'll be going back, and I wouldn't be surprised if we have a visitor from the island here with us soon."

Zoe laughed, remembering how eager Francis had been to come back through the door with them. Grandpa had had to convince him to wait until Sir Montrose and his men set sail back to England before any of the Robinsons considered going to the future. It would be hard enough to explain the sudden disappearance of Dave and the Hoisingtons, but it would be even more difficult to explain if Francis left with them. Besides, it would have been a terrible shame for him to miss Ernest and Elizabeth's wedding.

Had it really only been three days since Zoe and Katie had discovered the door in the tree? Of course, it felt much longer, but one thing was certain . . . life would never be the same again!

The End

Continue the Adventure!

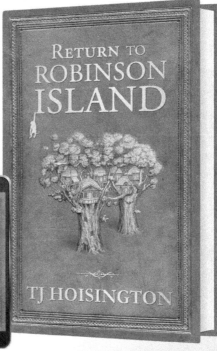

Book, eBook, and Audiobook are available at major booksellers and online retailers.

Special quantity discounts are also available.

Please visit us at the website listed below.

www.SwissFamilyReturns.com

About the TJ HOISINGTON

TJ HOISINGTON is the author of the first *Swiss Family Robinson sequel* in over 100 years, titled, ***"Return to Robinson Island."*** TJ is also the author of the international bestselling book, ***"If You Think, You Can!"*** – *sold in 34 countries.* TJ is the author of ***"The Secret of the Slight Edge," "If You Think You Can! for Teens"*** and numerous *leadership, management,* and *high-performance* development resources and curriculums.

Connect with **TJ** *on social media:*

@tjhoisington

www.GreatnessWithin.com
www.facebook.com/tjhoisington
www.instagram.com/tjhoisington
www.YouTube.com/greatnesswithin

About the KYLA HOISINGTON

KYLA HOISINGTON is a 13-year-old entrepreneur, social media content creator, and she strives to be a positive influence on everyone she meets.

Connect with **Kyla** *on social media:*

Instagram @kylahoisington
YouTube @kylahoisington
TikTok @kyla.hoisington

Acknowledgements

Special thanks to all the reviewers and beta readers who read this book and gave valuable suggestions. We appreciate the ideas, candor, sacrifice, and energy you generously provided to help make this book a reality.

Thank you to the young readers: Paige Stoddard, Rebecca Spindler, and Mackenzie Sampson. Special thanks to Jeanette Withers, who read an early version and provided many ideas and suggestions. Thank you, Krisette Spangler, for your keen instinct for flow, authenticity, and deep understanding of historical time periods. We are deeply thankful for Jenny Parkin, who never ceases to amaze us with her writing and creative ability. She took each chapter and greatly enhanced the story from top to bottom.

We are thankful to you all!